PRAC
2/21

D1245237

COSPLAY
Killer

DAHLIA DONOVAN

HOT TREE PUBLISHING

ALSO BY DAHLIA DONOVAN

THE GRASMERE COTTAGE MYSTERY TRILOGY

Dead in the Garden - Dead in the Pond - Dead in the Shop

MOTTS COLD CASE MYSTERY SERIES

Poisoned Primrose - Pierced Peony

LONDON PODCAST MYSTERY SERIES

Cosplay Killer

STAND-ALONE ROMANCES

After the Scrum - At War With A Broken Heart

Forged in Flood - Found You - One Last Heist

Pure Dumb Luck - Here Comes The Son

All Lathered Up - Not Even A Mouse

The Misguided Confession

THE SIN BIN (COMPLETE SERIES)

The Wanderer - The Caretaker - The Royal Marine -

The Botanist - The Unexpected Santa

The Lion Tamer - Haka Ever After

Cosplay Killer © 2020 by Dahlia Donovan

All rights reserved. No part of this book may be used or reproduced in any written, electronic, recorded, or photocopied format without the express permission from the author or publisher as allowed under the terms and conditions with which it was purchased or as strictly permitted by applicable copyright law. Any unauthorized distribution, circulation or use of this text may be a direct infringement of the author's rights, and those responsible may be liable in law accordingly. Thank you for respecting the work of this author.

Cosplay Killer is a work of fiction. All names, characters, events and places found therein are either from the author's imagination or used fictitiously. Any similarity to persons alive or dead, actual events, locations, or organizations is entirely coincidental and not intended by the author.

For information, contact the publisher, Hot Tree Publishing.

www.hottreepublishing.com

Editing: Hot Tree Editing

Cover Designer: BooksSmith Design

E-book ISBN: 978-1-922359-33-9

Paperback ISBN: 978-1-922359-34-6

For my husband, who lost the bet and owes me a hundred bucks.

"I'm Oz. He's D. And we'll be back for another rundown of murder and mayhem next week. Stay tuned for Osian and Danny's London Crime Podcast." He checked his watch, counting down a few seconds before signalling to Dannel to pause the recording. "Another one bites the dust."

"Oz and D?"

Osian grinned over the top of his laptop at his boyfriend of fourteen years. They'd been best friends practically from infancy and started dating in their teens. "We're hip with the kids."

"I am not hip. I have two." Dannel swivelled in his chair before pushing himself across their living room floor. "And thirty isn't old age. Besides, how many teenagers are listening to true crime podcasts?"

"Let me have my dream." Osian followed him down the hall into their bedroom. He stretched out on the bed to watch Dannel prepare for his shift. "Ready to go for twelve hours?"

Dannel glared over his shoulder; his dark brown eyes always seemed to pierce into Osian. "What do you think?"

Truthfully, Osian didn't know for sure what Dannel thought about being a firefighter. Dannel had followed in his father's footstep, yet he didn't quite fit the mould. Osian worried it might come crashing down eventually.

Am I borrowing trouble from the future? Maybe it'll all work out on its own. Although, when does it ever?

Watching Dannel comb his short black curls trimmed into a high fade before spritzing his hair with argan oil, Osian couldn't help dragging his fingers through his own untidy brown mane. Though they had much in common, they were polar opposites in other ways. Their differences made their relationship stronger, in Osian's opinion.

Dannel always made him think of a buffer version of Richard Ayoade. Osian had a striking resemblance to the actor Matt Ryan. He'd even cosplayed as John Constantine and Edward Kenway because of it.

"Meeting me after shift for an early breakfast?"

"Go on, then." Osian leaned up on his elbows for a kiss. He smiled when Dannel brushed his lips quickly, then bolted from the room. "Bye."

Since they'd grown up together, Osian knew the ins and outs of Dannel's personality probably better than his own family did. They'd been inseparable from the time they could toddle across the hall to each other's homes. He'd been the first one Dannel told about his autism diagnosis.

With Dannel gone for his shift, Osian faced the silence in their two-bedroom flat with a sense of dread. He hated the quiet. It allowed his thoughts to stray to things better left forgotten.

Rolling off the bed, he headed into the en suite to stare glumly into his own blue eyes in the mirror. He shook his head. *I'm not old enough to feel so bloody tired all the time.* His thoughts seemed to drain every ounce of energy out of him.

Tired and drained.

Drained and tired.

Guilt weighed him down, as though the entire Tottenham Hotspur team had climbed on his shoulders. *Time heals all wounds is such bollocks.* A year hadn't brought him much relief.

When Osian closed his eyes, he remembered with agonising clarity every second of the night that changed his life. He'd been on shift with Gemma, driving their ambulance toward an accident not far from Stamford Bridge. They'd arrived to find the worst scene of their careers as paramedics. Abra had been there as well, partnered with Archie.

A Mini hatchback had tangled with a lorry; the latter had definitely come out the winner. The air ambulance had been unable to fly because of bad weather in South London. They'd bustled one of the two critical patients into their vehicle and taken off for the hospital.

Despite deft driving and fevered prayers, Osian hadn't held out much hope. He'd desperately weaved his way through the heavy traffic while Gemma did her best with the young woman. The crash victim had been barely clinging to life.

She'd coded two miles from the hospital, and Osian had pulled over immediately. He and Gemma had gone above and beyond to revive her. They'd succeeded, initially.

Once she'd begun to breathe again, Osian dove for the front seat. He made record time to the hospital. All their efforts had been fruitless; the young woman had died in surgery less than an hour later.

Osian had walked away from his dream job and

never looked back. He hadn't handled the loss well. *I failed her. We did.*

No matter how many times his counsellor told him that he'd done his best and circumstances had been out of his control, Osian knew it hadn't been enough. A young woman had died in his care.

His paramedic colleagues had all understood. They'd faced similar moments of crisis within themselves when the weight of the job became too much to bear. His family and friends had, for the most part, been confused by his decision.

Don't you love the work? You spent so much time studying to be a paramedic; why waste it? What are you going to do now? Even a year later, Osian didn't have answers to their questions.

The emails weren't helping, either. Not long after starting his podcast, anonymous messages accusing him of being a murderer had shown up. Osian saved them in a folder, trying not to let them affect him too much.

Needing to throw himself into something—anything —else, Osian had worked on his podcast. He and Dannel were obsessed with true crime shows. It hadn't seemed like a massive leap to talk about them online.

His mum and dad thought he'd thrown his education away. Osian knew they'd come around eventually. He'd already begun to make money with ad revenue and sponsors, plus the podcast kept his mind away from his failures.

The heat from the radiator drove him to shove his head out of the living room window. Osian breathed in deeply, allowing the crisp February breeze to wash over him. A shout from below caught his attention.

"Off for an adventure?" Osian waved at the familiar grey-haired couple and their tiny Yorkie, Thames. "How's the little beast doing?"

"We're going to Nordic Bakery. Fancy a bun?" Stanley asked, while Adelle, his wife, lifted Thames to wave his wee paw up at Osian.

"I wouldn't want to be a bother."

"We'll take that as a yes, duckie. We'll pop in when we return." She ignored his protests as he knew she would. "A Tosca cake and a hot chocolate with a shot of espresso coming right up for you."

Days like this, Osian adored living in Covent Garden. Their eclectic, colourful building matched the off-the-wall neighbours inhabiting it. He did occasionally wish they'd picked a newer place instead of one built right after the Second World War—mostly when repairs were needed.

It was also the only place Osian had lived, outside

of his flat in university. His family had lived across the hall from Dannel's. When his folks and later Dannel's mum had moved away from London, they'd taken over one of the four apartments in the building.

The flats and the shop on the ground floor were owned by Dannel's uncle Danny and his auntie Myriam. They continued to refuse any offer of rent. "Not from you lads, we couldn't" was the familiar refrain from the two.

Myriam and Danny had always been supportive of Dannel. When his dad had left, his uncle had stepped in to be there for his namesake—Myron Dannel York. It had still been rough on the twelve-year-old, who hadn't understood adult relationships.

With his strained relationship with his dad at the time, Dannel had chosen to go by his middle name instead of his dad's. He had more or less reconciled with Myron, the elder, in his twenties. The name had stuck.

"Ring a ding ding."

Osian shook his head at the call that followed the knocking on the door. He went over to greet Stanley, who handed over a paper bag and his coffee. "Let me—"

"Don't be silly." Stanley cut him off before he could even offer a tenner. "Will you be coming by for the communal curry night? It's at Ian's, since young Evie and Dannel are both on duty at the fire brigade."

"I wouldn't miss it," he promised.

Once a week, they had a themed meal night in the flats. Evie Smith lived in the apartment across the hall that had once held the York family. She was Dannel's best friend, and his uncle had cut her a deal on the rent. They worked together as firefighters.

The last of the tenants, Ian Barrett, was the eldest in age and had also lived in the building the longest. He'd been there before the Orteas had taken over management. A bit of a hermit while at home, he still came to the meal each week and flourished into a dramatic social butterfly when in a group.

"What am I even doing with myself?" Osian fished out the sweet almond Tosca cake. He wasn't surprised to see a berry bun underneath it. Adelle always spoiled him and Dannel as though they were her grandchildren. "Is a podcast really a career? Why am I talking out loud? We need a pet, so at least I can use them as an excuse."

At the age of thirty, Osian hadn't expected to have a mid-life crisis. His best friend and former paramedic partner, Abra, had told him all he needed was a reset. He hadn't found an on-off switch yet.

He returned to stand by the window and watched

people strolling down the sidewalk. *Chin up. Maybe something interesting will happen. But you can't hang around all day waiting for it to happen.*

Making a quick decision, Osian grabbed his mobile before he could change his mind. He phoned Abra while shoving his laptop into a bag. She readily accepted his invite.

The weather was deceptively beautiful outside; he might as well get some work done while enjoying the fresh air. Abra promised to bring a picnic. Osian shoved a mini bottle of wine into his bag and headed out to the gardens of a nearby church.

Of all the available open spaces, Osian loved the church gardens. They were quiet. No one ever bothered him there, not even the priests.

It probably helped that he and Abra had once been called out to help one of the elderly priests who'd suffered a stroke.

"Ciao." Abra hopped over the bench to sit beside him. She waved a container. "I brought snacks."

"Ciao? Really?" Osian shook his head, brushing her wild mane of curly hair out of his face. "I know you're Italian, but you don't speak a word of it. Who are you showing off for?"

"Spaghetti. Latte. Grande."

"Is latte Italian? I'm not sure food counts, or made-up Starbucks words." He grabbed the container and pulled the lid off to find mini potato pizzas. He couldn't remember what they were called, but she'd made them before. "Yum."

"Yes, latte's Italian, you numpty. I promised my nan I'd learn."

"Shouldn't that be your nonna, then?" Osian snagged one of the pizzas. "How's work?"

"Oz."

He held up a hand in surrender. "Just asking."

She narrowed her hazel eyes on him. "It's not the same without you. They keep having me train noobs. Think they're hoping you'll come back."

Osian clenched his fingers around the pizza. He forced himself to breathe. "Can't."

"*Bene*. Fine."

"So how much time are you spending on Duolingo?" Osian teased.

"It's like my judgemental mother. Messaging me at least once a day to ask if I've done what I promised to do." She accepted the paper bag he offered. "Oh! Tosca. You wicked man."

"Yeah, yeah. Read this." Osian twisted his laptop around so she could see the email. "Got this in the podcast inbox."

"Why don't you investigate the crimes of a paramedic murdering a patient?" Abra read the single line of the email. "What the...?"

Osian glanced up when she didn't finish her sentence. "Weird, right?"

"Distinctly odd."

2

DANNEL

Stepping out of the station after his twelve-hour shift, Dannel wanted nothing more than to slip into a warm bed and have Osian's arms wrapped around him. *Is one in the morning late or early?* London had turned cold, windy, and drizzly overnight.

Dannel waited outside for Evie. He leaned against one of the red metal shutter doors of the station. His patience started to run out just when she finally appeared. "Took you long enough."

Despite not technically being related to him, Evie's family came from the same neighbourhood in Jamaica as his dad's. They were practically cousins. They'd become fast friends during their firefighter training.

"Prat." Evie dragged a hat over her short black hair. She adjusted her green eyeglasses that always made him think of a cat's eyes. "Are we walking in this soggy mess?"

"Comic Con," Dannel shouted, drawing looks from a group walking across the street.

"Inside voice, Dan. Inside voice." Evie, like Osian, always did a great job of helping him regulate his volume. He rarely realised how loud he was getting and had asked them in the past to give him a heads-up. "And yes, I'm aware Comic Con is tomorrow. Is your costume ready?"

"Finished fabricating the last piece of my armour last weekend. Thought about growing my hair out a bit, but I'll just wear a helmet." Dannel hadn't wanted to deal with the fuss. He'd found having any length to his hair gave him massive anxiety. "My Liam cosplay might be the best I've done yet."

"Well, you look a bit like him." Evie had been as much of a fan of Liam from *Mass Effect: Andromeda* as Dannel. "What's the Oz-man going as?"

"Nathan Drake."

"Fitting. I've got the day off and my Commander Shepard outfit from last year. Might join you. Think there will be tickets to spare?" Evie strode down the pavement, forcing him to keep up with her. "What do you think?"

"About?" Dannel tried to pay attention, but the

flash of lights down the corner and the shouting from a nearby pub made it difficult. "What do I think about what?"

"Me? Buff, renegade Shepard?" Evie flexed her upper arms, showing off her muscles. "That's your yes face, right?"

"Sure." Dannel stared at his reflection in a shop window. "It's definitely an expression of some sort."

In truth, Dannel didn't know. He struggled to decipher body language, emotions, and tone of voice. His —and others. His expression seemed suitably blank.

Why do they say know thyself?

How do I know myself?

I barely figure out what I'm feeling while it's happening —half the time Ossie has to help me decipher it.

Maybe it should be, get a boyfriend who knows you, so you can know thyself?

"Hey, you hungry? Evie grabbed his sleeve when he continued forward after she stopped. He let her guide him across the street. "I'd sell your soul for nuggets."

"My soul?"

"I figure I'm worth chips, nuggets, and a shake." She grinned. "Are you up for a late-night or early-morning snack? My protein bar didn't even take the edge off my hunger."

"You know protein bars aren't good for you."

"Not taking nutritional advice from a man who drinks milkshakes every day of the year." She darted through the sliding door in front of him. "I'll pay, since you treated yesterday."

"I've bought our after-work snack for ten days in a row." Dannel waved woodenly at the cheerful young man at the register. They were regulars at their favourite late-night spots. "Milkshake—half chocolate, half vanilla. Three large chips. And whatever she wants."

Be more polite.

Dannel tried for a smile, though it felt more like a grimace. "Thanks."

"Thanks" is polite, right? Is it the right word? Why is this so hard?

"He means. Hello. How's your night gone? We're absolutely shattered. Too many wankers out there setting fires and making work for us." Evie flashed a better example of a welcoming grin than Dannel could ever manage, no matter how much he practised. "We'd love two large shakes, two large chips, a cheese melt sharebox, spicy nuggets, and sweet chilli chicken wrap."

"Hungry?" Dannel blinked at the larger than normal order.

"You know Oz-man's going to want the wrap for breakfast." Evie had an excellent point. "We'll eat the melts on the way home."

Another excellent point.

At the end of a twelve-hour shift, Dannel wanted two things—silence and food. On busy days, they tended to not have time for meals. And he constantly struggled with sensory overload.

He hated it.

Hated how his struggles made him feel like a failure when he logically knew he wasn't.

"What's with the frowny face?" Evie nudged him away from the counter. She handed over his milkshake and the box of melts, keeping the bag with the rest of the food under her arm. "Let's get you home. You're definitely more worn out than I thought."

He didn't argue.

"Dannel?"

"What?" He glanced over at her.

"You could quit."

He shrugged. "I'm aware of the possibility."

"There's no shame in changing careers in your thirties." Evie chewed on a chip. She had one of the packets in her hand and held it out to him. "Oz-man would support you. So would I."

"Yeah." Dannel snagged a few greasy chips. "My dad would be disappointed."

"The man who walked out when you were a kid and only came back when you were a teenager?" Evie held a grudge far longer than he did. She was a good friend. "I think it's all in your head. No one would be disappointed if you stopped being a firefighter. I'd miss you, but honestly, we live in the same building. I'd see you every day, no matter what. The stress isn't worth it."

What could he say? The job everyone thought was his dream job made him beyond miserable. It sent his blood pressure soaring just picking up his gear.

It wasn't the work itself. Or not only the daily grind of potentially life-threatening situations. The constant racket at the station between sirens, co-workers, and engine noises combined with dealing with people non-stop made life hell. He wondered how many years had been knocked off his life from the damage of the high-stress environment.

"Why don't you chat with your Oz-man about it?" Evie wrapped her arm around his shoulders. "I love you, so I'm not afraid to say being stubborn over this is beyond senseless."

"I know."

They finished the chips and cheese melts on the

walk home. Evie disappeared into her flat. Dannel smiled at her door, then headed into his own.

Creeping quietly into their flat, Dannel froze at the sight of Osian asleep on the sofa. He'd obviously tried to wait up. The last few hours of a shift always made Osian anxious. They tended to be the most dangerous hours of his day. Tired firefighters and paramedics tended to make mistakes at the end of a shift. They were alert and aware at the beginning.

Dannel set his drink and the bag of food on the coffee table. "Ossie?"

Osian groaned into the cushion. He sat up and smiled groggily at him. "Home. Good. Sleep now."

He caught Osian before he could lie back on the couch. "Why don't you go to bed? You'll hurt your back out here."

"Smell chips," Osian muttered. He stretched his arms slowly, revealing the soft, pale skin of his stomach and the wisps of hair down his abdomen that Dannel loved. "Save me any?"

"And a wrap."

"I'm suddenly wide awake." Osian stood up and stretched for a second time. "Or, my stomach is."

Grabbing the bag, Dannel offered it to Osian. He went into the kitchen to pour a glass of water. His body wanted nothing more than to collapse in bed and not move for at least a decade.

Dannel moved over to stare out the window. He loved the silence of their street in the early morning hours—one of the positives of his late shift. "My ears are ringing."

Osian put the bag into the fridge and came up to wrap his arms around him. "Why don't we put the *Hamilton* album on? It always helps you relax. Or maybe your gaming soundtrack compilation?"

"Musical silence?"

"Musical silence."

Musical silence.

The term they'd come up with as teens. Osian had seemed to instinctually understand how music settled something deep inside Dannel. They'd spent endless hours on the roof of their building, listening to their favourite albums and ignoring the world around them.

"My vote's for *Hamilton*." Dannel tilted his head to rest against Osian's shoulder. The arms around him tightened. "Cold chips and salty political quips."

"Punny."

"I thought so." He breathed in deeply; just being home with Osian eased some of the tension in his body. "Tired."

And he was. Evie had been right when she'd said he needed a change. He simply didn't know how to make the first step.

"Do you want to talk about it?" Osian hesitated when Dannel immediately shook his head. "Okay. Greasy chips and music it is."

3

"If we don't answer, they'll get tired of knocking and go away," Osian whispered. He peered through the peephole at his baby sister, Olivia, and Dannel's younger brother, Roland. Both twenty-seven, both constant annoyances to their older siblings almost from birth. "They're together. Never a good sign."

"Bugger." Dannel stepped up behind him. He leaned against Osian, pressing him into the door so he could look through the peephole himself. "Maybe they'll get bored if we ignore them."

"Inside voice." Osian groaned before chuckling. He had no doubts their siblings had heard Dannel. "They might've brought a bribe."

Knock.

Knock. Knock.

Knock.

"They could at least tap out a rhythm." Dannel winked at Osian, who laughed against Dannel's shoulder to muffle the sound.

"We can hear you laughing." Olivia calmly interrupted their snickering fit. "We brought cake."

Dannel glanced toward the door. "Cake?"

Osian tried to silence him with a searing kiss. "We aren't that easy."

"What kind of cake?"

"Made a Bakewell Swiss Roll."

Dannel opened the door so fast it that he almost knocked a laughing Osian to the floor. "Sorry, Ossie."

"Yeah, yeah, get the cake before they drop it." Osian waved off the unnecessary apology. "Apparently, we are easy enough to be bought by pastry."

"Cake." Olivia handed over the plate to Dannel, who immediately made a beeline for the kitchen with his younger brother on his heels. "You'd think no one ever feeds them."

"I shudder to think about how Auntie Rolina managed to feed both of them without going bankrupt. Remember when they hit their growth spurt in their teens? They practically inhaled food." Osian draped an arm across his sister's shoulders. "How are you doing, kid?"

"First, you ate as much as both of them." Olivia dug her elbow into his side. "Second, I'm only three years younger than you."

"Still a kid to me." He paused when she held him back.

"How are you doing?" His sister ignored the sounds of the now duelling brothers, fighting over the cake with extended forks they'd been given as a joke gift ages ago. She always read him better than everyone else. "Osian?"

He never knew what to say. There were no easy answers. Olivia tended to read him better than anyone aside from Dannel, so faking his way through a lie was pointless.

He ran his fingers through his hair, tugging on the ends. "Better? Not perfect. Still a few rough days here and there where I hate myself."

"Better is good. Better without the question mark would be *better*," she teased. "Wish you'd let us help."

"I'm—" Osian was cut off by a loud crash in the kitchen. "They dropped the cake. Thanks, you know, for bringing a homemade pudding for me. The floor really appreciates the thought."

"Should we help?"

He glanced at the jumbled mess of broken ceramic, frosting, cake, and jam. "How about no? They broke it, they can figure this out."

They made the mistake of meeting each other's gaze and immediately collapsed into hysterical laughter. It took ten minutes to calm down. And infinitely less time to clean up. Osian mourned the cake dumped in the rubbish bin.

"So, leftovers?" He pulled out the pizza box from the bottom of their fridge. "Got enough for a slice each."

Cold pizza. Colder beer. They lounged in the living room, eating, drinking, and arguing about the best musicals. The passionate debate ended with Osian and Dannel loudly re-enacting their favourite song from *Wicked*—out of tune.

"Why exactly did you two come over?" Osian pulled Roland aside while Olivia and Dannel cleaned up from their impromptu party. "It wasn't this."

Roland folded his arms across his chest, and the smile evaporated from his face. "Your sister is persuasive."

"You're a hardened detective."

"I haven't quite made detective." Roland flicked him on the arm. "Have you talked to Evie lately?"

"Why?" Osian glanced over at Dannel, who'd put

on his headphones. *Time for the siblings to go. He's definitely reached his limit of socialisation.* "Can you summarise for me?"

"You're not the only one in need of a change of career." Roland nodded towards his older brother. "Think about it."

The siblings headed out after a bit. Olivia had a class to teach in the morning and a husband working the late shift. Roland gave Osian a pointed glare before following her out of the flat.

Osian grabbed his phone from the counter to text Evie, only to be immediately distracted by a new email. "What a bellend."

Another anonymous letter, almost exactly the same as the last one.

Tapping his finger against the side of his phone, Osian wondered why the anonymous messages set him so on edge. He'd tried tracking the email. There was no concrete identifying information.

A faceless wanker hiding behind technology who made Osian's head hurt.

Maybe I should send these to Roland? Coppers investigate things, right? He can play detective and figure this out.

"Ossie?"

Osian followed the voice down the hall to find

Dannel holding two pieces of the harness that made up part of his cosplay. "What happened?"

"Your sister or my brother." Dannel gently set the broken straps down on one of the tables. They'd turned their spare room into a workspace. "Hand me the glue—not the wood one but the fabric one."

"Ahh, yes, clear concrete." Osian dug around in the tall cabinet to find the right bottle. They'd taped over the real labels and come up with names of their own. "Think it'll hold?"

"Long enough for the convention. Unless you want to be *Hamilton*? Again." Dannel kicked the stool closer to the table. "Not sure I'm down to be Washington. The breeches itched."

Osian grinned to himself. He hadn't minded the breeches on Dannel. The costume had clung to his body in wonderful ways. He had a lot of pleasant dreams about those trousers.

Right, focus on this year's costume.

I can't be Nathan Drake without a weapon harness.

Drawing his mind away from thoughts of Dannel dressed up, Osian gathered up a few scraps from when they'd made the harness. They kept the leftover pieces for repairs. He set a few on the table within easy reach.

Osian watched Dannel deftly piece his costume

back together. "Want to model last year's outfit for me?"

"Not wearing itchy breeches for you."

"What if I make you non-itchy ones?" Osian pushed his luck.

"Maybe." Dannel kept his attention on the harness. "Grab my thin pliers?"

"Needle nose?"

"Thin," Dannel insisted. "I like my word better."

"An adventurer and a space cop walk into a bar."

"This isn't a bar," Dannel corrected. He shoved his hands into his pockets; stress made always seemed to make him more pedantic. "I hate this."

"I know." Osian wrapped an arm around his shoulders—awkwardly, given the armour of his costume. "We can hang out here for a while."

Cosplay had been one of Dannel's greatest passions for a long time. They'd been to so many conventions. And every time, he had a meltdown on the walk there.

Not always on the walk. Sometimes on the Tube. Occasionally at home before.

He'd push through, like always. And he'd be

exhausted afterwards. Most of the time, he thought the entire exercise was worth stress and strain.

Then, other times, Dannel wondered how many years the strain would take off his life. He feared eventually he'd have to stop attending conventions. His health might begin to be seriously affected by the stress.

Okay. Morbid thoughts are morbid. Shake them off. I love cosplay. All our friends are here. We're dressed up. Ossie is hot as Nathan Drake. I can do this, even if I just stare at his arse the entire way. It's a useful distraction.

I can do this.

Dannel repeated his internal mantra until his breathing settled. "Ready?"

Osian eyed him for a second before handing over the helmet part of his Liam Kosta costume. "We can go home, you know?"

They could. Dannel would regret it. He breathed in deeply and settled the helmet under his arm.

Courage occasionally came from donning a character.

"Let's have fun." Dannel grabbed Osian's hand. "We skipping the queue?"

"Gemma and Ethan wanted help setting up the first aid booth." Osian guided him past the regular entrance, flashing their badges to security. "I promised we could play assistance."

"Free tickets?"

"Free tickets."

Gemma Cox had been Osian's on-and-off partner as a paramedic. She'd traded off with Abra and Archie, another paramedic friend. Ethan was her current beau. They were part of a small but devoted group of London first responders who enjoyed cosplay.

"Boys." She waved them over with a grin, barely shifting her focusing from setting up their portable defibrillator. They'd crowdfunded for it a few years back after someone had a heart attack in the middle of a Star Trek Q & A. "Oz, give me a hand with this?"

Dannel went over to Ethan to allow the two former paramedics to handle their business. "Need anything?"

"Help me get these freebies on the table? We decided to hand out survival kits with water and other essentials. Hopefully, we'll have fewer cases of dehydration. You'd think people would be aware they can't spend an entire day wandering around without having a drink of something." Ethan used his foot to nudge one of two plastic bins toward him. "Are you two planning on staying here when the doors open or checking out a few panels first?"

"Panels."

"Panels? Good choice." Ethan shifted away, turning his attention to the second container. "Right."

What do I say next?

Setting his helmet to the side, Dannel turned his attention to the little packets. Ethan seemed content to work in silence. He appreciated his friends knowing when small talk wasn't necessary.

By the time the doors opened to let the flood of people in, the first aid station was ready to go. Dannel and Osian snuck away to get to the first of the question and answer panels. They'd waited all year to be up close and personal with the angel and demon from *Good Omens*.

"Will you be okay on your own?" Osian followed him out of the conference room when the panel finished. "I promised Gemma I'd check in with her. Have you heard from Evie?"

"She slept in. Typical." Dannel didn't honestly expect any of their friends to go to the first day of the convention. They usually came on the second. "Go on. I'm starved. Want me to grab a snack for us?"

Osian leaned over to kiss him over the front of his helmet. "Have fun."

The best thing about a convention was being able to put a helmet on—and have people ignore him. He got fist bumps and high fives. Conversation was irrelevant.

No one was there for Dannel. They loved his Liam Kosta cosplay. They were there for the character.

What was I thinking?

The lines for any of the food vendors practically went the length of the building. Dannel gave up. He didn't need to eat that badly—Gemma and Ethan probably had snack bars and water left.

He arrived at the first aid station to find Abra and Evie seated behind the table. He poked his best friend in the arm. "You couldn't text me?"

"I brought sandwiches and coffee." Evie tossed a wrapped packet at him. "Forgiven?"

"Sure." Dannel hooked a chair with his foot to ease it out from under the table. He sat heavily and yanked his helmet off. "Remind me to vent this better next time."

"Steaming up in there?" Abra grabbed a cup of coffee from a drink carrier. "Where's your lesser half?"

"He said he was going to be here. Haven't you seen him?" Dannel felt his chest tightening when Abra shook her head. He stretched his arms out, careful not to spill his drink or dump the sandwich. "Shoot him a text?"

"Already sent him three." Abra paused to slap a Band-Aid on a paper cut on Wonder Woman's finger. "Complete radio silence."

His appetite vanished. The food he'd eaten churned in his stomach. Dannel knew Osian well enough to know he'd never ignore multiple texts.

They'd worked as first responders long enough to know how no response could cause a great deal of concern. Dannel set the sandwich and drink on the table. He grabbed his phone and called Osian.

It rang.

And rang.

Dannel disconnected the call when it went to voicemail. He glanced over to his right and spotted missing equipment. "Where's the defibrillator?"

"No idea. Ethan didn't know when we showed up. He assumed Gemma had it." Evie had her mobile out as well. "None of them have replied to my messages."

Anxiety ate at him like a monster in his gut. Dannel got to his feet. He'd never known Osian to ignore all of them.

"Where is he?"

"Inside voice, Dannel," Evie reminded him.

"Bugger my inside voice." Dannel strode away from the table. "I'm going to find him."

Weaving through the crowds filling the halls, Dannel doggedly made his way toward the security office. He knew they had rows of CCTV cameras. They'd hopefully be able to help him find Osian or call for him over the tannoy.

Surely Osian wouldn't ignore that as well?

Halfway to security, Dannel spotted cluster gathered outside of one of the rooms. He froze when paramedics pushed by him toward the doorway. The churning in his stomach increased, and he followed after them.

The room was utter chaos.

The defibrillator had been tossed across the room and broken into several pieces. Osian was on the floor frantically doing CPR on someone. Dannel squeezed through the crowd of onlookers to find the lifeless form of Gemma.

What the bloody hell happened?

"Ortea. Get your man, will you?"

Dannel nodded at one of the paramedics he vaguely recognised. He knelt down to wrap his arms around Osian. "Come on, Ossie. Let them help her."

"I can do this. I can." Osian fought against him,

struggling to get back to their friend. "Won't lose another one."

Dannel clutched him tightly to his chest. "It's going to be alright."

It wasn't, but Dannel didn't think either of them wanted to face the truth just yet. He'd seen enough dead bodies over the years as a firefighter. Nothing was going to bring Gemma back to them.

"Let me go. I can save her." Osian tried to break away from him.

Dannel, being taller, broader, and certainly stronger, forced Osian over to a corner of the room. "Easy, Ossie. Don't."

"Not again."

He didn't quite know how to help his boyfriend. Nothing he said would make him feel better, but he tried anyway. "I'm so sorry."

5

OSIAN

This is a nightmare. It's a nightmare. I'll wake up covered in sweat, again, and everything is going to be just fine.

No matter how hard Osian tried, the image of finding his friend lifeless on the floor wouldn't get out of his head. He rubbed his eyes with the heel of his hand, trying to force the tears back.

Why can't I ever save anyone?

The police had arrived not long after the paramedics. They'd cleared away the gawkers but insisted Osian and Dannel stay behind. After Gemma had been taken away, the two had been separated by constables.

"Mr Garey?"

"Osian." He peered up at the detective who'd introduced himself as Haider Khan. "Just Osian."

"Mr Garey. Can you walk me through what happened?" Detective Inspector Khan appeared to prefer a measure of professionalism. He sat in one of the fold-out chairs across from Osian. "Take your time. I know this is hard."

"Do you?" Osian reeled back in his sarcasm. It wasn't the detective's fault his friend had died. "Sorry, sorry. I came back to the first aid table, but Ethan said Gemma had gone off with the defibrillator. I went to find her to see if I could help. She was just... there on the ground. Not moving. It was dark in the room. I flipped on the lights, rushed over, felt for a pulse, called 999, and then began trying to resuscitate her."

The detective jotted a few notes into his notebook. Osian tried to read them upside down. Haider Khan had worse handwriting than any doctor he'd ever seen.

Osian found himself staring at the spot on the floor where Gemma had been. He blinked when the detective called his name. "Pardon?"

"Did you touch the defibrillator?" Detective Inspector Khan repeated his question.

"No." Osian considered the question. "This morning, I did. I helped Gemma get it set up, but not later. It was across the room when I came to check on her."

"You remember that?"

Osian paused in his recollection to stare pointedly at the detective inspector. "I worked as a paramedic for a long time. We're trained to quickly assess situations. When I found Gemma, I thought I might need to use the defibrillator. It didn't take more than a second to realise someone had broken it."

"Any thoughts on who?"

He bristled at the detective's tone. "Not a clue. As I said, she was alone when I got here. She certainly wouldn't have broken the defibrillator herself. It cost us too much to get."

Detective Inspector Khan leaned forward toward him. "Did you kill her?"

"Have you lost your sodding mind? Did I kill her?" Osian went from shocked and irritated straight into incandescent rage. "She was already—" Clenching his fists, Osian pounded a hand against his chest. The room felt smaller, tightening around him. He couldn't breathe.

"Mr Garey? Mr Garey?" Detective Khan reached out hesitantly to touch his arm. "Should I call for paramedics?"

"I'll be fine." Osian shook his head rapidly. He

forced himself to count to ten and then backwards to zero, breathing shakily with each second. "Sorry. Gemma was one of my best mates. I'd sooner have jumped into the Thames than hurt her."

The detective waited until Osian's breathing sounded better to continue. "Is there anything else you remember?"

"No, not really." He slowly relaxed his hands and settled into his seat again. "I don't understand what happened. Why would someone hurt Gemma?"

"You were a paramedic? Familiar with the equipment in the room?"

"Yes. Familiar enough to save a life." Osian didn't want to think about any of it. He wished he could walk out of the room. "Why?"

"Could you kill with it?"

"Me, personally?" Osian reared back, offended by the suggestion. "I may not be a paramedic anymore, but I always considered my job was to save lives."

"Humour me?" Detective Inspector Khan prompted.

"The machines have fail-safes. They're not supposed to discharge without analysis of a need." He tilted his head to the side, considering all he'd learned over the years. "Unless the wiring had been messed with, I don't see how it could've killed. It shouldn't shock without the presence of a particular type of heart rhythm. Gemma's was fine, I assume. She didn't have any issues I'm aware of. Ethan might know better."

"There's no manual override?"

"Not on this model." Osian had checked it over himself earlier when they'd been setting up for the day at the first aid table. "I don't know enough about the mechanics of the machine itself to tell you how tampering would affect its ability to function."

"Where were you before the incident?"

"With my boyfriend. We'd gone to one of the show panels. I decided to check in at the first aid table while he went to find food. I told you this already." He scrubbed his fingers across his eyes. He wanted to nap for a million years until the pain in his chest went away. "Am I a suspect?"

"Not at the moment. We're pulling the CCTV footage. Timing will be everything." Detective Inspector Khan stood up and handed over a card. "Call me if you think of anything. We'll be in touch. Don't leave the city, will you?"

Blinking in confusion at the card in his hand, Osian walked woodenly toward the door. He was struggling to process. Dannel waited for him outside, leaning against the wall across from the room.

Dannel rushed forward, wrapped an arm around him, and walked purposefully down the hall. "I'm calling Roland."

"What's he going to do?"

Dannel kept a firm hold on him. "Calling Roland."

"Why? He's not a detective. He can't do anything."

"Yes, but calling Roland means getting to Wayne more quickly." Dannel practically dragged him through the convention crowds toward the line of taxis. He shoved Osian into the back of one and muttered the address to the driver. "You're getting a solicitor."

"I haven't done anything wrong. I don't need a solicitor." Osian wasn't overly concerned about the detective inspector's questions. They'd been standard, in his opinion. He had been the one found in a room with a body. "It's going to work. They have CCTV footage. They'll be able to see when I went into the room."

"I'm calling Roland." Dannel crossed his arms and stared stubbornly out the window. "How many cases have we seen of an innocent person getting convicted? No. Wayne will help."

"Dannel."

"*Ossie.*"

He knew that tone of voice intimately. Dannel

could dig his feet in and refuse to be moved when he wanted. There was no point of arguing with him when his mind was made up.

"Why don't you text your brother? He's not on shift tonight. Invite him and Wayne over. I'm sure they'd love to have an excuse to get together." Osian had watched with amusement as Roland and his closest friend from university danced around each other. He'd dated men and women over the years, but Wayne was his storybook true love. Their timing had never been right. At least, that's how it appeared from the outside. "We'll grab a takeaway."

"It's the bottomless pit of a stomach that masquerades as my brother."

"We'll get a lot of takeaways."

Dannel shifted until they were leaning against one another. He grabbed Osian's hand tightly. "You'll have a solicitor."

"Not arguing." Osian rested his head against Dannel's broad shoulder. "Didn't even ask about Ethan. He must be gutted."

"I didn't see him."

Osian sat up and glanced over at him. "What do you mean?"

"He vanished before I went to find you." Dannel shifted beside him. "Didn't see him anywhere, not even when the detectives were rounding everyone up to ask questions."

"Weird."

Incredibly weird. Why would he vanish? He knew I was going to find Gemma.

The drive to Covent Garden from the convention seemed to take forever. Dannel wanted to scream directions at the driver. London traffic, though, wasn't for the faint of heart.

Their cabbie wasn't trying to be difficult for the fun of it. They'd simply picked a bad time of day to rush home. He settled into the seat with a hand resting on Osian's knee, trying to offer some small measure of comfort.

Grief was strange, a mercurial monster that Dannel didn't know how to approach.

After what seemed like a century, the cabbie pulled up outside of their building. They paid him, ran up the stairs to their flat, changed out of their costumes, showered together, and collapsed on the couch in sheer emotional and physical exhaustion. And Dannel still didn't know what to say to Osian.

Their friend had died. Osian had once again been faced with a situation where even his best herculean efforts hadn't saved a life. No words would make him feel better.

"What did Roland say?" Osian broke the silence in their apartment first.

"Don't talk to the detectives without a solicitor again." Dannel paraphrased his brother's advice toward the end of their lengthy text conversation. "Or ever."

"They aren't going to railroad me." He was more confident than Dannel felt.

"It's not about them. A solicitor has your interests at heart. The detectives have a case to solve." Dannel loved his brother and uncle, both of whom worked or had worked in the police force. He didn't have blinders on when it came to all of the various cases they'd studied for the podcast, some involving innocent people who'd been convicted erroneously. "We're not taking any chances. I believe they'll do their best to find the killer. I'm not risking you on the off-chance they make a mistake."

They lapsed into silence again. Dannel was starkly reminded of the weeks immediately after Osian had quit work. He was sad about Gemma, but he couldn't do anything for her now.

She was gone.

Osian, on the other hand, was alive and suffering. Dannel wanted nothing more than to alleviate his pain. He didn't feel equipped for the task at hand.

Should I call Abra? She knows both of them. Maybe she'll know what to say.

"Ossie?"

Getting no response, Dannel decided to handle ordering food on his own. Most of the time, Osian made those calls when required. Dannel tended to get tongue-tied trying to talk on the phone.

Thank the internet gods for online ordering.

When Roland and Wayne showed up, they'd run into the delivery person and brought the food up with them. Dannel gestured with his head toward Osian, who hadn't moved from the couch. He figured maybe they could help with more than just the legal aspect.

"Thanks for the invite, mate." Wayne carried one of the bags with dinner over to the kitchen. "I'm happy to help any way I can."

"Ossie?" Dannel called over to Osian, who hadn't bothered to great their guests. "You joining us?"

"Not hungry." Osian shifted off the couch and disappeared down the hall.

Shifting from one foot to the other, Dannel didn't know how to approach his boyfriend. Should they leave him alone? Or force him to come out to sit with them?

"Go talk to him." Roland nudged his brother into action. "We'll get the food set up. Make sure you're patient with him."

"I am," Dannel insisted. "I haven't pressed him once for anything."

Roland held his hands up. "I know, big brother, I know. Not an accusation, man."

Dannel watched his brother through narrowed eyes for a few seconds. "Fine. Sounded like an accusation."

Leaving the two in the kitchen, Dannel went to retrieve Osian. He found him flopped on top of the bed with the *Uncharted* soundtrack playing. His arm covered his face.

Dannel sat on the edge of the bed closest to Osian. He hesitated before reaching out to grasp his boyfriend's hand. "I want to help, but I don't know how."

With a watery chuckle, Osian slowly sat up. He kept a firm grip on Dannel's hand. They sat in silence for a minute, broken only by sniffles.

"Roland can come back later." Dannel had no

doubt his brother would complain, but he'd go anyway. "He'll whinge, which is nothing new."

"Be nice to your baby brother. We might need someone on the inside if I get arrested." Osian managed a less watery laugh. "They came all this way. The food will get cold."

"We have a microwave."

"Not the point." Osian rested his head against him. "Also, inside voice."

"Yeah, yeah, yeah." Dannel tried hard to moderate the volume of his voice; it never seemed to work. He had two modes—quiet and loud. "So? Dinner?"

"And beer. We'll raise one for Gemma."

Dinner and beer sounded amazing. For Dannel, the entire process was overwhelmingly uncomfortable. He'd overextended his ability to deal with people, even his loved ones, for the day.

Trying to listen to the conversation floating around, Dannel couldn't filter out the sounds of eating and drinking. The cacophony of noise drowned out any words. He rubbed his forehead with a quiet groan.

"I—" He cut himself off, not knowing how to express himself. Words seemed to vanish no matter how hard he tried to hold on to them to form sentences. "Ossie."

"Why don't you get some quiet time? I'll deal with

these two muppets." Osian proved once again how well he knew Dannel. "Love you."

Muttering a response, Dannel was the one to flee down the hall this time. He grabbed his noise-cancelling headphones, turning on one of his favourite gaming playlists and relaxing in the darkness of their bedroom. The day had been too long, too overwhelming for his sensory issues; he wanted musical silence until the buzzing in his mind went away.

They didn't need him to brainstorm anyway. He couldn't really put sentences together at the moment, even if he wanted. *Am I getting to the point where I can't go to cons anymore?*

Just thinking about not being able to attend conventions again devastated Dannel. For one, it was something he and Osian enjoyed so much as a couple. He'd thrown so much of his life outside of work and his relationship into cosplay.

It wasn't fair.

7

OSIAN

"O z-man."

Holding his hand up, Osian silenced Roland. He wanted to give Dannel enough time to get his headphones on. They didn't need to exacerbate the situation.

He could kick himself for not grasping how crushing the day had likely been for the love of his life. On a good day, a convention tended to be beyond exhausting for Dannel. Adding the intense emotional weight of a murder had to amplify the feeling tenfold.

"You were saying?" Osian prompted after a minute or two.

"I'm sorry about Gemma." Roland clinked his glass against Osian's bottle. "How serious do you think the detectives were when they talked with you?"

"There was a dead body involved. How serious do you think they were?" Osian pushed his chair back from the table, stretching his legs out with a groan. "Detective Inspector Khan had a lot of questions for me. I got the idea he might have more."

"They'll consider you a suspect but also a witness as the first person on the scene. They will most certainly have more questions for you," Wayne interjected into the conversation. "You've got my number. The second they call you, I'm the next person you talk to."

"I'm innocent."

"And? It has nothing to do with guilt or innocence." Wayne leaned forward with his elbows on the table. "While I have the utmost respect for our police force, my job is to ensure you understand the questions and don't accidentally incriminate yourself for something you haven't done."

"Wayne." Roland flicked a bottle cap at his lawyer love interest. "Really? Really."

"Are you going to try to tell me innocent people aren't talked and bullied into confessing?" Wayne took a sip of beer before staring Roland down. He shifted his gaze over to Osian. "You call me, alright?"

Osian gave a sharp salute. "I'm sure it's not necessary."

"You call me."

"Just say you'll call him, because he won't shut up if you don't," Roland exclaimed.

Osian had to smile when the two fell into a playful argument. His amusement faded when his phone buzzed in his pocket. "Abra?"

"I just heard."

He felt the dizzying sickness in the pit of his stomach once again. "I meant to text you."

"I can't believe it." She sounded devastated. "Are you okay?"

"I'm alive, so yeah."

"Oz."

"What do you want from me?" Osian moved away from the table for a façade of privacy. "She died in my arms."

"Did she, or was she already gone when you got there? Don't let your mind mess with you." Abra spoke firmly. "I know you want to believe we have the power of life or death, but you can't raise the dead."

Osian forced himself to think about the events of the day. "She wasn't breathing."

"There you go, then."

"Yeah, listen, can I call you later? Roland's here with a friend." He ended the call with a muted good-bye. He glanced up to find the two men cleaning up the leftover mess on the table. "You don't have to do that."

They ignored him. He'd known they would. Roland and Wayne left after cleaning up, once again reminding him to call if the detectives had more questions.

Despite everything, Osian wasn't worried about himself. He drifted over to sit on the couch and stare at the black screen of the telly. His mind refused to let go of one important question.

Who killed Gemma?

And why?

"Ossie?"

He tilted his head and saw Dannel in the hallway. "You okay, love? They're gone. Want to join me in contemplating the blank telly?"

Dannel rolled over the edge of the couch, winding up on his back with his head in Osian's lap. "Are we going to the convention in the morning?"

"Do you want to go?" Osian hadn't even thought about the second day of Comic Con.

"I asked first."

"It wouldn't be the same." Osian hated the idea of wasting all the time and effort they'd put into their costumes, but he couldn't imagine enjoying the day when all his thoughts would be turned toward the loss of their friend. "No, I don't want to go."

"Me either." Dannel closed his eyes and yawned. "We should podcast."

"Wait. What?"

"Podcast Gemma's murder. Interview Ethan. Talk to the detectives."

"You want me to have a chat with them?" Osian stared incredulously down at Dannel. "Not sure that will take me off the detectives' radar."

"You're innocent," Dannel stated pragmatically.

I know I'm innocent.

You know I'm innocent.

Not confident the coppers will care or appreciate either of our opinions.

Deciding not to debate the matter, Osian shifted down the couch, closing his eyes. Dannel had a stubborn tendency to view justice as crystal clear. Osian knew how muddied the waters could get.

They fell asleep on the couch. Exhaustion, grief, and worry had taken their toll. Osian woke to find Dannel rushing around, having been called in last minute to cover a shift at the fire station.

He barely got a kiss on the lips before Dannel vanished out the door. "Well, okay then."

An hour later, Osian hadn't moved off the couch.

He finally made himself get up and shower. The heat of the water helped clear his head enough to get something more than staring at the wall accomplished.

He still had a towel around him when the detective inspector called and requested he come in for a few additional questions. *Well, damn.* Trying not to assume the worst, he dressed quickly and called Wayne. The solicitor insisted he wait for him.

Osian stood outside the police station with two coffee cups in hand. He'd wanted something strong and sweet for himself and grabbed a second for Wayne. *Stop panicking; they don't have anything. It's just questions.*

"Oz-man." Wayne jogged down the street toward him. He was trying to fix the knot on his tie while awkwardly holding a messenger bag under his arm. "Shall we?"

Osian hid his grin behind his coffee cup. "You've got a massive hickey on your neck."

"Shit."

"Have a good night with Roland, then?" He headed up the steps with Wayne following close behind. "Need me to help with your Windsor knot?"

"Shut up."

"Yeah, I'm feeling really confident about you helping the police take me seriously." Osian watched while Wayne finished with his tie. He straightened up, all signs of humour and his easy-going attitude vanished, leaving a serious, competent solicitor behind. "Coffee?"

Wayne grabbed the spare cup. "Let's not make the detectives wait."

They stepped up to the front desk, introducing themselves. The constable at the counter directed them to take a seat. Wayne led him over to the row of uncomfortable seats lining the wall.

"How's Roland?"

"Oz." Wayne elbowed him in the side. "Focus."

The two bantered back and forth. Wayne continued to deflect his inquiries. Osian couldn't wait to text Dannel about his baby brother's romance with their solicitor friend.

"Mr Garey."

Osian glanced up to find a new detective, a woman. He didn't remember seeing her at the convention. "That's me."

"Detective Inspector Powell. If you wouldn't mind following me? We're set up down the hall for a little chat." She turned her attention to Wayne. "You brought a friend."

"Wayne Dankworth." He smiled charmingly at the

detective. "Mr Garey happens to be a close friend as well as a client."

The detective inspector seemed to reconsider what she'd been about to say. Instead she turned, inviting them to follow her. Osian clutched the cup in his hand and tried to calm his racing heart.

Inspector Powell paused at a door, gesturing for them to step inside where Haider Khan waited for them. "If you'd both have a seat?"

There's no need to stress. I didn't do anything. I'm a witness. Nothing else.

The two detectives had definitely decided to play good cop, bad cop. They alternated peppering him with questions, often repeating themselves. Wayne kept a calming hand on his shoulder; he'd squeeze gently whenever Osian seemed to be getting worked up by the intense interview.

Interrogation.

It's definitely more interrogation than a casual interview.

"Mr Garey? If you could answer the question." Detective Inspector Powell pushed the printed image of Gemma across the table. "You were the last person to see her alive. What happened?"

Osian shook off the hand on his shoulder and leaned forward with his elbows on the table. "I was *not* the last person to see Gemma alive. When I found her, she'd already breathed her last breath. Nothing I could've done would've made a difference. I have no idea what happened. If I did, you'd be the first to know. I don't appreciate the veiled implication. She was a good friend. I have no doubts the CCTV shows when I headed toward the room."

"We found your fingerprints."

"I performed CPR. You likely found my DNA on her as well." Osian ignored the shifting Wayne to his right. "My costume left my face clear for any cameras in the area. So, not to repeat myself, but CCTV should show the time I arrived in the room."

The detectives continued their probing questions about his history as a paramedic and working with Gemma. They asked about Ethan and Gemma's ex-husband. Osian wondered how long they intended to drag this out; he didn't see how any of his answers would lead to a murderer.

Unless Ethan did it.

"What is it, Mr Garey?" Detective Inspector Khan asked. "You've remembered something."

Osian blinked a few times, trying to process the change of tone. "Maybe. It's something Dannel, my boyfriend, mentioned to me on the way home."

"Which is?" Khan prompted.

"Ethan disappeared." Osian scratched his jaw, trying to remember. "Ethan pointed me in the direction Gemma had gone. And was gone when Dannel went to the booth looking for me. How could he vanish despite knowing something had happened to her? We both found it strange. They'd been dating for a while. You'd have to drag me away kicking and screaming if our situations had been reversed."

"And this is Ethan Stewart? Also a paramedic?"

Osian bristled at the tone. He didn't need the touch of Wayne's finger to his arm to know he needed to take a breath. "We're all part of a cosplay group made up of first responders—police, firefighters, paramedics. We're family. No one would want to hurt Gemma. She was a sweetheart."

"Someone obviously did." Inspector Powell jotted something down in her notebook. She tapped her pen against the page. "How was your relationship with the victim?"

His day hadn't been particularly long or stressful. It had been an average one at the station. Most of his anxiety had come from waiting to hear back from Osian about his visit to the police station.

They hadn't arrested him. Osian had texted the second the interview had wrapped up. The detectives definitely considered him a suspect, but hopefully his willingness to talk put him low on the list.

Both Wayne and Roland had messaged him. They'd wanted to assure him Osian was fine. Dannel had finally switched off his phone to avoid the constant beeping from the incoming texts.

Stepping out of the station, Dannel dragged on his hat. He'd missed Evie. She hadn't taken an extra shift, so he'd been without his best friend for the day.

"Son?"

Dannel was surprised to find his dad waiting for him at the end of his shift. "Myron."

Closing his eyes, Dannel took a few deep breaths. He honestly didn't have the energy to deal with drama. Myron brought drama with him even when he didn't intend to.

His father always flinched a little when Dannel called him by his name. "How are you doing?"

"Fine." Dannel shouldered his bag and adjusted the beanie on his head. "It's late in the day for you to be hanging around the station just to ask how I'm doing."

Take a breath. It's been a long day. Don't snap at him before he's been a pain in the arse.

"The café across the street is open. Why don't we grab a coffee and chat?" Myron gestured toward it. "Shall we?"

"I want to go home. I'm tired," Dannel muttered stubbornly. "Ossie's waiting."

"He can wait." His father crossed his arms. "Just a coffee."

"Fine."

With a belaboured sigh, Dannel tried to walk off

some of his irritation. He wanted to go home. His plan had been to walk straight there.

The plan had changed.

He didn't like plans changing on him. It tended to throw him completely off-axis. His family were often the ones to do so most frequently.

"Your uncle saw Osian at the police station." Myron waited until they'd gotten their drinks to get to what was clearly the point of his visit. "Is he in trouble?"

And instead of calling me, he nattered on the phone to you.

Why?

Why do they always do this?

"A friend passed away. They had questions since he attempted to resuscitate her." Dannel frowned at his coffee. He didn't really want caffeine this late at night. The café didn't serve milkshakes—and his dad had thoughts about what men drank. "You came all this way for that? Why not text me?"

"You never answer your phone," Myron pointed out.

"If you didn't insist on calling instead of texting, you might have better luck." Dannel answered his phone for his mum, Osian, and his job. "Messaging is a perfectly valid form of communication. Better, even, since I have less chance of misunderstanding."

"Dannel."

"*Myron.*" He set his cup aside, completely disinterested in the coffee. "I don't understand why you came all this way."

"You're my son."

"Not actually an answer." Dannel scratched his head, then readjusted his beanie. "I'm going home. I'm too tired to decipher what you want."

"I worry. Your friend passed away. Your whatever you want to call him is a suspect. I'm a father. I'm allowed to show concern." Myron reached out to grip Dannel by the shoulder. "You could at least make eye contact."

"No, I can't." Dannel shrugged the hand off his shoulder. His frustration with his father increased at the man's consistent inability to understand him. Eye contact made him intensely uncomfortable, and he listened better when he didn't have to stress about it. "Thanks for the coffee. I should head home. Osian worries if I'm late."

"You don't need a nanny." Myron had never liked Osian even when they were younger. "How many blokes are there in London? You couldn't pick someone with sense. I could set you up on a blind date with a perfectly respectable man."

"What?" Dannel didn't know which part of his dad's argument he found the most illogical. "Ossie's not my nanny. A blind date? What the bloody hell are you on about? I'm attached at the hip to the man I've loved since before I knew what falling in love even meant."

A nanny?

Honestly.

What kind of absolute nonsense is he going on about?

His career wasn't exactly the safest. Something his dad knew intimately as a retired firefighter. *This is the last thing I want to deal with after the week we've had.*

"And for your information, Ossie worries because I risk my life on a daily basis running into fires." He abandoned his untouched coffee and stormed out of the café. "Why do I bother?"

Dannel jogged across the street. His relationship with his father always seemed to be two steps forward and ten back. They never managed to stay on the same page.

As a result, Dannel usually wound up feeling like a constant source of disappointment. He got the impression he could never match up to his younger brother in their father's eyes. It was exhausting.

Despite his best efforts, his dad caught up to him. Dannel ignored his presence. He walked stubbornly in silence, finding the shortest and straightest path to their flat.

"Son?"

Dannel plodded on without saying anything. His temper had started to flare, and as always, much to his added frustration, his mind decided to forget how to put sentences together. He needed to be home.

"Son."

Despite what some of his family believed, Dannel didn't run from arguments. He required space to process. His dad continued to follow him all the way to his building.

"Hello, love. Where were you? I was worried you and Evie got lost. Ahh, Myron." Osian was lounging on the couch in a T-shirt and sweatpants. He got to his feet quickly when Dannel came in with his dad following. "What a pleasant surprise."

"Bed." Dannel continued through the flat into their bedroom, slamming the door behind him. He fell face-first onto the mattress and muffled his scream of frustration into a pillow. "I hate words."

Rolling all the way down the bed, Dannel reached out to grab their Bluetooth speaker. He paired it to his phone and quickly scrolled through his playlists.

Breathing came a little easier to the strains of *The Hamilton Mixtape.*

By the fourth track, Dannel had released some of his stress. He shifted onto his back to stare up the ceiling. The voices in the living room had gotten quieter; he trusted Osian to deal with Myron.

Trusted him to handle everything, really.

The moment Dannel rushed into the flat. Osian had known something was wrong. His gaze immediately turned to Myron when he stepped into their living room.

"Myron."

"Osian."

Osian reminded himself that getting into a fistfight with Dannel's dad probably wouldn't solve anything. "A little late to be chasing your son to his bedroom."

"If he'd learn how to handle conflict, I wouldn't be following him down the street." Myron stepped further into the living room. "He's a grown man."

"What did you do?"

"I don't like your tone."

"I like my tone just fine. You storm into our home

when you've obviously upset Dannel—not sure you get to comment on how I speak to you." Osian had once been scared of Myron York, but he wasn't a little kid or a punk of a teenager anymore. "What did you want with him anyway?"

"You were arrested."

"No, no, I wasn't." Osian lifted both arms up. "See? No handcuffs. I was simply helping the detectives by answering a few questions."

The conversation danced around for several minutes. Myron asked questions. Osian artfully avoided answering them.

Their chat bordered on a hostile interrogation from both sides. They'd never gotten along. Myron had taken an instant dislike to him and never changed his mind.

He'd completely tuned out the man when something caught his attention. "What did you say?"

"You're coddling him."

"And you hate how he loves and respects me more than he's ever done you." Osian thought if he'd been an attack dog, he'd have gone for Myron's throat. He despised the way the man treated his son. "So, you've overstayed your welcome. The door is behind you. Why don't you see yourself out of it?"

Myron's jaw practically hit the floor. He didn't

seem to be able to put together a response. His fists clenched tightly at his side, and Osian prepared himself for a fight.

Crossing his arms, Osian stared down the taller and larger man. He had no desire to play the polite game. Family might be family, but Dannel would always come first for him.

Always.

After several long minutes of uneasy staring, Myron backed off and stepped out of the flat. He slammed the door behind him, not unlike his son had done earlier. Osian dropped onto the couch with a tired groan.

Save me from overly dramatic men who slam doors and won't talk about their feelings.

At the heart of it, Osian knew Myron cared deeply for his son. He simply didn't appear to know how to express his love. It left the two at odds more often than not.

Heading to the kitchen, Osian fixed two mugs of tea and grabbed an opened packet of biscuits. He tucked the latter under his arm, managing the cups in his hands. With a little deft work, he got the door open.

It wasn't a surprise to find Dannel listening to one of his favourite albums. Osian set the mugs on one of the nightstands. He tossed the packet onto the bed and flopped down beside it.

"He gone?"

"Yep." Osian twisted on his side. He plucked the biscuits up before he crushed them. "Hungry?"

"Tired. I could manage a biscuit." Dannel snagged a couple and sat up to eat. "Or an entire tin."

"We've got a packet." He was relieved to see some of the tension gone from Dannel's shoulders. "Almost a tin."

Shifting further, Osian rested his head against Dannel's thigh. He brushed at the stray crumbs dropping on his forehead with a chuckle. Dannel grabbed his phone to adjust the volume of the music playing.

"So, how many lectures am I getting about being nicer to Myron?" Dannel spoke after inhaling his fourth Bourbon biscuit. "Your tea's getting cold."

Osian gave an exaggerated groan before pushing himself up into a seated position. He snagged his mug and handed the second one to Dannel. "Who's going to lecture you? Not me. Probably not your mum. Roland? If he actually runs to his youngest son to whinge about my telling him off, I'd be genuinely surprised. Your baby brother doesn't pick sides."

It had always surprised Osian how Roland managed to avoid all family drama. He never chose sides. It was irritating at times when he didn't step in to defend his brother.

Then again, Osian had a rather skewed perspective. He'd fight any number of people on his sister's behalf. They were fiercely protective of each other.

Holding his mug carefully in his left hand, Osian stretched out his right to gently grasp Dannel by the back of his neck. He tugged him forward into a kiss. They separated after several minutes.

"Love you." Osian took a sip of his tea and snagged one of the last Bourbons to dip into it. "Are you feeling better?"

"Always with you."

"Remember your podcast suggestion?" Osian switched subjects, pausing to let Dannel process the change. They'd dealt with family nonsense enough for the rest of the month. "Investigating Gemma's death?"

"I don't think I suggested investigating." Dannel repeatedly coughed to clear his throat of the biscuit that he'd clearly inhaled. "*Ossie.*"

"What?"

"We're not shoving our noses all the way in the police's business," Dannel warned.

"Better to investigate and find answers than have them dragging me in for questioning repeatedly because I was the last person in the room." Osian didn't quite believe he was completely off the police's radar. "At the very least, I want to chat with Ethan. Isn't it odd how he vanished?"

"Very." Dannel finally nodded his agreement. "Fine. I've got the next few days off. How about we pay a little visit to Ethan?"

Ethan. And track down Noah, Gemma's ex, to see if he's returned from his extended self-imposed exile.

A jealous ex-lover wouldn't be a complete stretch as a potential murder suspect if he were in the city.

"We can stop by on the way to Olivia's." Osian glanced over when he didn't get a response. Dannel had slumped over and already begun to snore. "Sleep well, love."

Lifting the packet of biscuits, Osian tossed the last one in his mouth and dropped the plastic into the rubbish bin. He made sure both of their mugs were safely out of reach. They'd knocked over too many glasses over the years; he didn't want a rude awakening with broken mugs and tea everywhere.

Again.

Despite the soothing music and the familiar rhythm of Dannel's breathing, Osian found sleep difficult. He'd covered them both loosely with a blanket. His head rested on Dannel's chest while he contemplated the mystery of Gemma's death.

The broken defibrillator kept popping into his mind. It had been an older model—one they'd been able to easily afford for their group. While it had safety precautions to prevent accidental discharge, anyone with the right knowledge could circumvent those and overcharge the equipment.

It wouldn't be outside of the realm of possibility for someone to use it to stop Gemma's heart.

But why? Why Gemma? What could she have possibly done?

The question stayed on his mind even as he drifted to sleep.

The following morning, Osian snuck out of bed. He left Dannel still sleeping. His eyes kept trying to close on him while he brewed a fresh cup of coffee.

Midway through his second cup, a sharp whistle outside caught his attention. Osian stepped over to the window and stuck his head outside. He frowned at his brother-in-law, who was waving enthusiastically up at him.

Morning people.

"Why don't you come up?" Osian rolled his eyes when Drystan waved him down instead. "Fine. Hold on a second."

Glancing down at his T-shirt and sweatpants, Osian decided Drystan could deal with him in his sleepwear. He took the steps two at a time. By the time he reached the ground floor, Ian Barrett, their seventy-six-year-old neighbour and infamous rogue who worked as a consultant for a local theatre troupe, was chatting up his brother-in-law.

"Ahh, Osian, who's this lovely dish whistling up at your window like a young Romeo?" Ian draped a lanky arm across Osian's shoulders. "You must introduce me."

"He's married, Ian."

"I've had married men."

"He's married to my sister." Osian tried not to laugh at the look on Drystan's face. "Aren't you late for the morning rehearsal?"

Ian tapped the side of his nose and shrugged elegantly. "Fair enough. You two misbehave. I always do."

"Drys." Osian turned to him once Ian was out of sight. "Shouldn't you be fighting fires or throwing rose petals in front of my sister while she's walking?"

"I'm on my way home. Your darling sister wanted me to make sure you two were doing alright." Drystan sounded genuinely concerned, so Osian held back his sarcastic response. "Are you two okay?"

"You could've texted me to ask."

"You're well versed in the art of lying via text. But

you don't have a poker face to save your life. So asking in person seemed the best option." Drystan held a hand up to stop Osian from responding. "I can see you're at least not eating your way through every chocolate biscuit in the shop. And we wanted to make sure you're coming over for Sunday roast."

"On Monday. Why don't we call it Monday roast?"

"Osian."

"Mum," he teased.

"Don't be a prat." Drystan shoved him away. "We'll see you this evening, then. Try not to get yourself arrested in the meantime."

"Ha. Ha. Ha."

"I promise we'll have cake. We can hide in the corner, eating it while Olivia, your mum, and Dannel's mum argue about whether cereal constitutes soup." Drystan grinned with him. "Wait? Are you wearing pyjamas? Honestly."

"Tell your wife that we're fine." Osian dragged his brother-in-law into a hug, then sent him on his way. "And quit hanging out under my window. Someone might get the wrong idea."

"Prat."

"I made a list."

"What?" Osian shifted closer to look at Dannel's phone. "Of course you did."

"How else are we going to remember the questions for Ethan?" Dannel had used jotting them down to distract himself from family drama. He'd spent much of the bus ride making notes on his phone. "Can you think of anything else?"

"You were thorough." Osian scrolled through the twenty-plus questions. "Incredibly thorough."

"Are you laughing at me?"

"Only on the inside." Osian winked at him, blocking his arm when Dannel went to elbow him in the side. "So, you hold him down, and I'll interrogate him."

"We can't hold him down." Dannel pocketed his phone and shifted in the uncomfortable seat. He hated taking the bus. "Think he'll answer our questions?"

"He will if you hold him down." Osian snickered with him. He twisted his head to the side to brush his lips against Dannel's mouth. "He might. What're the most important things we want to know?"

"If he killed Gemma."

"Inside voice, love." Osian pinched the bridge of his nose. "Maybe we should be a little more circumspect?"

"Why?"

"Because non-autistics need subtlety. We don't deal well with blunt queries." Osian stretched his legs out, making Dannel envious of his smaller stature. He wasn't quite as squashed as Dannel. "We prefer reading between the lines of conversation."

"But why? It's so pointless," he grumbled. "We could save so much time."

Despite being surrounded by non-autistics and being in love with one, Dannel didn't know if he'd ever be able to understand them. Life was so much simpler when people said what they thought and got straight to the point. The subterfuge exhausted him.

What's the point?

Why can't we just walk up to Ethan and ask him?

Osian nudged him gently with his elbow. "I know what you're thinking. The reason we can't simply ask him is not only will he not tell us the truth, it'll probably cause him to shut down. He won't answer any of our other questions. If he didn't do it, he might have a piece to the puzzle. We wouldn't want to make him clam up at the first hurdle."

"Hurdle?"

"Metaphor."

"I understand what a metaphor is. Yours doesn't make sense," Dannel argued.

"Sure, it does. I'm the king of metaphors."

"Metaphors aren't a territory. How can you rule over a verbal concept? Or would it be a construct?" He batted away Osian's second attempt at a kiss. "No public displays of affection. Sometimes people get weird."

"Sometimes people are rude wankers. Let's get back to me being the Tsar of Metaphor."

A few stops later, they were hopping off the bus, still debating Osian's metaphor. They made their way to Gemma and Ethan's place. The two had moved in together only a few months ago.

"What if he's not home?" Dannel glanced down

the street. "Hey, we're not far from the tattoo shop. Want another one?"

"More toast?" Osian grinned.

They both had a number of tattoos. They had matching jam-covered toasts with smiley faces on their ankles. Osian had the PlayStation controller buttons down his calf designed like an inkblot test along with a rendition of the *Assassin's Creed* logo.

Aside from the jammy toast, Dannel only had one other tattoo. He had a stylised firefighter helmet on his back. It was a memorial for a friend lost on a call a few years back.

"Not sure there's space on our to-do list for an impulsive tattoo session." Dannel pointed down the street. "Ethan."

"I see him." Osian whistled sharply, which immediately got his attention. "He doesn't seem thrilled to see us."

"Not a requirement." Dannel followed Osian, who jogged down the pavement to catch up to Ethan. "I'm never thrilled when visitors show up unannounced."

"Which is why no one does."

"No one does because you get shirty on my behalf when they do. And I love you for it." Dannel had always appreciated how voraciously Osian defended his need to be in control of his environment. "Hello, Ethan."

Ethan glanced between the two of them uneasily. "Surprised to see you both in my neighbourhood."

"Gemma's neighbourhood," Dannel commented absently and blinked a few times when Ethan physically recoiled. "We're happy to see you too."

Ethan rubbed at his eyes. He motioned toward the building behind them. "Why don't we grab a coffee? I somehow doubt this is a coincidental meeting."

They got coffee and snacks, then headed across the street to the park. Ethan seemed content to wait them out. He sipped his drink, staring at them expectantly.

"How've you been?" Osian asked.

"Fine."

"Why'd you run off when Gemma died?" Dannel peered over at Osian when he smacked him on the arm. "What?"

"Subtlety."

"I didn't ask him if he killed her," Dannel protested.

"*Dannel.*" Osian covered his face with his hands and burst out laughing.

"What?" Dannel had stuck to the rules.

"If you two wankers are quite finished?" Ethan

scowled at them with his coffee cup clutched tightly in his hand. "I'm still grieving, you know?"

"Not an actual answer." Dannel ignored the hand Osian placed on his arm. He knew the police wouldn't completely remove Osian from their suspect list until they'd solved the murder. Why dance around the issue? "Where'd you go?"

"I panicked." Ethan was definitely not using his inside voice. "The police already asked me. I felt like I was suffocating, and I ran outside. She was gone. Going into the room wouldn't have done a thing to help. I can't resurrect the dead."

"Why not come back when you felt better?" Osian asked while Ethan seemed to be trying to calm himself down.

"It felt too real."

"I made a list of questions." Dannel redirected the conversation slightly. He didn't want Ethan to clam up on them. "Just a few."

Ethan began to pace in front of them. "Well, go on then. I can't exactly stop you if you want to play detectives."

"Were you arguing at all? Had any recent fights?" Osian stepped in, despite his claims about wanting to be subtle.

"No," Ethan said heatedly. "We had little spats like every couple but nothing recent."

"Who would want to hurt Gemma?" Dannel had a feeling any more pointed questions about Ethan's involvement would end their conversation. "She didn't do this to herself."

"How would I know? Everyone adored Gemma." He shoved his free hand in his pocket and waved the coffee cup around with the other, sloshing some over the side. "Wait. No. She'd heard from Noah recently."

"Noah?" Osian sat up on the bench. "Didn't he move to Cornwall?"

"He moved back." Ethan shrugged. "He was trying to worm his way into her life again."

"Was he?" Dannel knew Osian had considered Gemma's ex. He hadn't personally known him well, though Osian had worked with him on occasion before the break-up and move. "Was he stalking her?"

"She never said. I just know he'd left a few messages." Ethan tossed his cup into a nearby rubbish bin after spilling coffee for a second time. "Why don't you ask him your questions? I'm going to be late. Her parents have scheduled the memorial for the end of the week. They wanted to make sure you both knew. Are you going?"

"Of course." Osian shook his hand cordially.

Dannel simply waved. He stretched his legs and then got to his feet after Ethan had disappeared. "Not sure this trip was worth it."

"Well, what have we learned?" Osian grabbed his hand and led him through joggers in the park. "He told us about Noah."

"He wanted us to know about Noah. To focus on him." Dannel grabbed Osian with his other arm to keep him from falling when his foot caught on the side of the kerb. "He was very insistent that they weren't arguing."

"Too insistent," Osian agreed. "I went through my texts with Gemma from the last month. The ones to just me and the ones to our group chat. In hindsight, she seemed stressed."

"Aren't we all?" Dannel sidestepped a mum trying to wrangle two toddlers on the pavement. "Adulting equals stressed."

"More than the average level of anxiety." Osian paused when they reached the entrance to the Tube station. "Right. Are we going to the family dinner or home to relax and nosh on leftovers?"

"You want to face our mums when we ghost them?"

"Family dinner it is." Osian kept a hold of his hand

while they manoeuvred through the afternoon crowds. "Maybe we should've gotten a cab."

Part of Dannel did want to go home or at least grab a cab. He didn't have much left in him to handle the crowded train ride. And family dinners weren't exactly quiet with their loud, rambunctious families involved.

No matter how much their mums claimed to understand when they begged off the weekly dinner. Dannel always felt guilty. He'd push through, then spend time recovering when they got home.

As the carriage got increasingly crowded, Dannel regretted their decision not to grab a cab. It definitely would've been preferable to being jostled around. He felt like someone had shoved cotton into his ears—sounds were distorted by it.

"Dannel?" Osian tugged on his hand. "This is our stop."

"Right."

Getting to their feet, they rushed out before the door shut on them. Dannel pulled his earbuds out and dropped them into his pocket. Osian followed him down the platform, up the stairs, and out into the suddenly grey skies.

They wound up jogging through the pouring rain. Olivia waited for them by the front door with two large towels. Dannel grabbed one gratefully, listening to his mum clicking her tongue at their lack of an umbrella.

Who carries a brolly around on a sunny day?

When was the last time I even had one?

Do we own one?

Olivia inspected them while they tried to dry themselves off in the foyer. She grabbed both of them by the hand to drag them down the hall into her spare room. "You should both fit Drystan's T-shirts. Poor Oz might drown in them a little. Let me grab you something to change into, and we can throw your wet clothes into the dryer."

"Pushy bint." Osian grinned, then dodged out of the way of his sister's punch. "Thanks, kid."

"Brothers." She shook her head at him. "Don't strip yet. I don't want to see your bits."

"*Sisters.*"

After a few minutes, Olivia waltzed back in with the clothes. She tossed them at her brother, then left, closing the door behind her. Osian simply rolled his eyes.

"Sisters. I don't recommend them." Osian changed out of his clothes quickly. He eyed Dannel as he stared blankly at a photograph on the wall. "Why don't you take a nap? Bed's comfortable enough."

"I'm an adult."

"And? Adults don't nap?" Osian had obviously recognised how close to the edge of a shutdown he was. "I'll turn out the lights. You plug in your earbuds and listen to a soundtrack. Food can wait."

Dannel hesitated for a moment. "Okay."

He bent forward to brush his lips against Dannel's. "Love you."

"Go on, Ossie. Before our mums decided to come help us."

"Lose someone?" Olivia was waiting for him by the door to the kitchen. "Did Dannel need a rest?"

"He did." Osian held his arm out for him to loop hers around. "We had a long day."

"Oh?"

He shook his head as they stepped into the kitchen. He had no interest in alerting his mum or Dannel's to their inserting themselves into the investigation. "I'll tell you later."

Olivia tapped her nose and winked at him. "Sibling cone of secrecy."

"What are you two whispering about?" His mum narrowed her gaze on him. He dragged Olivia in front of him. "You're both taller and wider than your sister. Quit using her as a shield."

"Is she calling you short or me fat?" Osian grunted when she elbowed him in the stomach. "What? Mum said it, not me."

"Behave." His mum whacked him lightly on the shoulder with her spatula, then wrapped her arms around him. "What happened to Dannel?"

"He's resting," Olivia offered while Osian went from one hug to another as Dannel's mum welcomed him. "He'll eat later."

"And what did you do to my Danny?" Dannel's mum glowered playfully at him.

Dinner thankfully distracted both of their mums from Dannel's absence. Drystan and Roland showed up in time to eat, as per usual. Osian inhaled his meal, trying to politely leave to check on Dannel without insulting anyone.

He wasn't overly concerned. Dannel came first in his mind—always. Family understood.

Or, if they didn't, they'd learned not to pester him about it.

Osian stepped into the spare room to find Dannel stretched on his back, staring up at the ceiling. "Couldn't sleep?"

"Thinking about Noah and Ethan." Dannel rolled over on his side. "I should get up."

"You could." Osian dropped onto the bed beside him. "Or we could stay here and hide until everyone leaves."

"Olivia would sneak food in for us."

"She definitely wouldn't let you starve." Osian knew his sister adored Dannel and had already squirrelled away a plate for him. "Sadly, I think they'll come searching for us eventually."

And they did.

The family crowded into the guest room after fifteen minutes. They'd brought pudding. A dark chocolate roulade. It perked Dannel up enough to endure being fussed over.

After another hour of family bonding, Dannel gave Osian "the look." He knew it well. It was the one that meant the love of his life had officially reached the end of his rope.

They made a quick escape, hopping into a cab for the ride home. Osian hadn't wanted to risk another crowded trip on the Tube. He wasn't surprised when Dannel immediately fled into their bedroom.

Osian stayed in the living room. He could hear the strains of one of Dannel's favourite soundtracks playing. "One of these days he'll stop pushing himself so hard."

Grabbing his laptop off the table, Osian collapsed onto the couch with a groan. He kicked off his shoes. *Right, let's see what old Noah is up to lately.*

Osian had barely gotten into Facebook when his phone buzzed. "Abracadabra."

"Oz-man. Heard you riled up a hornets' nest."

Osian stretched his arm out to grab his headset, allowing him to put his phone down and continue perusing the internet. "Who, me? Would I rile someone up?"

"Your existence riles people up. Who are you trying to kid?" Abra chuckled. He heard her telly going in the background. "Rumour on the paramedic grapevine is you were asking Ethan a lot of questions."

"Really? Ethan was talking about it?" Osian had expected him to avoid everyone. "I'm surprised."

"He seemed to want to ensure we all knew he thought either you, Dannel, or Noah killed Gemma." Abra had always enjoyed a good gossip session. Then again, nothing stayed secret between paramedics. They spent too much time together. "Did the police really accuse you of murder?"

"No, no, they didn't. He's stretching the truth." He wondered how badly their brief questioning had shaken Ethan. "Well, he's going back on top of my suspect list."

"Your suspect list? This isn't one of your podcasts, Oz. You're going to get yourselves in trouble."

"I'm trying to get myself *out* of trouble," Osian insisted. "What are you doing tomorrow?"

"Osian."

"Aren't you the least bit interested in why Noah has suddenly returned to London?"

"What?" Abra shouted so loudly he had to pull the phone away from his ear.

"Are you kidding? After all the drama when he ran off?"

"Nope, I heard it straight from Ethan." Osian wondered why Ethan hadn't mentioned that during his attempt to deflect attention away from himself. "Dannel's on shift tomorrow. Why don't we go on an adventure?"

"If you get me arrested...." She trailed off her warning.

"It'll be fine." Osian had no intention of drawing attention to himself. "We'll avoid imperial entanglement."

"Nerd." She laughed. "Fine. I'll come around nine. We can grab brekkie together."

Tossing his phone to the side after she hung up,

Osian returned his attention to locating Noah. He didn't want to ask Ethan. The man had clearly been ticked off at their questions.

Noah Rose.

It didn't take long to find him on Instagram. *I should've known.* Noah had curated quite the account for himself, all glitz and glamour. All photos of his adventures in Europe. Noah looked more like an Instagram model than a paramedic. Osian wasn't at all surprised.

Of all their co-workers, Noah had definitely bordered on arrogant when it came to his body and appearance. Osian had wondered if his ego hadn't been able to take the hit of being dumped. Gemma had handled it as gently as possible, but still.

No one enjoyed a break-up.

No one.

From his most recent posts, Noah had clearly moved into a swanky penthouse. *How on earth is he affording his rent? Is this fake? Would he Photoshop his life?*

Definitely.

Smarmy wanker.

If he's not, how the hell is a paramedic affording all of this?

After hunting through a few more photos, Osian

realised Noah had reconnected with several of their mutual friends. He grabbed his phone and quickly texted one of them. They gladly offered up Noah's new number and address without questioning why he wanted the information.

I just want to catch up with an old friend... and accuse him of murder.

Maybe I won't mention that part.

Calling Noah an old friend was a bit of a stretch. They'd been cordial to one another. He'd rubbed Osian the wrong way on several occasions with little snide comments about patients.

The majority of people who worked with the ambulance service believed in handling their injured patients with respect and care. Noah often stepped outside the bounds of their code, in Osian's opinion. Maybe that was why he could so readily believe him capable of murder.

Here's hoping we find him at home and feeling chatty tomorrow.

The following morning went by in a blur. Dannel had woken up twenty minutes late and run out the door, barely remembering to get dressed. Osian had taken his time getting ready.

Abra showed up an hour after Dannel had left, knocking repeatedly and grinning when he yanked the door open. "Morning, Oz-man. Ready to play copper?"

"Is there coffee for me?" Osian gratefully accepted the cup she held out to him. "Shall we? Ready for the Tube?"

"Not a chance. The Uber should be here in a minute, so hurry up." Abra grinned at him. "I refuse to deal with sweaty men at this hour on public transportation."

"Are there any hours you want to deal with sweaty men?"

"*Oz.*"

"What?" He grinned.

After locking up the flat, Osian raced down the stairs with Abra. He waved to Ian, who was on his way out as well. They thankfully didn't have time for a natter with him.

"So?" Abra asked expectantly when they'd slid into the back seat of their Uber and had ensured the driver knew where they were headed. "How are we going to get Noah to confess all his sins?"

"I'd settle for one." Osian shifted uncomfortably. His legs were awkwardly squashed against the driver seat. "Appeal to his ego?"

"It is Noah, so it wouldn't surprise me if stroking his ego does the trick." Abra flicked Osian on the arm when he snickered. "Get your mind out of the gutter. You know what I meant."

Their driver dropped them off a few streets away from where Noah lived. They'd wanted the walk to assess the situation. Or so Abra had claimed. Osian knew she was having second thoughts.

Confrontation was *not* one of her strong suits.

"Oz." Abra grabbed his arm, keeping him from rounding the corner. "Isn't—"

"Noah." He cut her off when he spotted what had drawn her attention. "Bugger. Well, time to put your acting skills to the test."

"What acting skills?"

Osian caught her by the elbow and propelled her forward across the street. They walked quickly to catch up with Noah, who appeared to be heading toward a parking garage. "Play along."

"This was a terrible idea." She shook her head.

"Noah? Noah Rose," Osian called out cheerfully. He plastered a smile on his face when the man in question turned around. "How've you been, mate?"

"Good?" Noah frowned at him. He definitely didn't seem thrilled to see either of them. "Osian. Abra. I don't usually see you two wandering around these streets."

Osian suddenly remembered why he'd avoided

Noah so much. The man made him want to wipe the smarmy grin off his face. *Please sir, can I have some more? Don't be an arse, Oz.* "Have you heard about Gemma?"

Noah's smirk evaporated in an instant. He breathed out sharply and shook his head. "The police informed me. Ethan told them that I'd held a grudge."

"Had you?" Abra asked.

"No, you...." Noah trailed off. He crossed his arms tightly over his chest. "I moved on—and up. I had no use for Gemma. Why the hell would I hold a grudge? I hadn't thought about her in months. And I certainly had better things to do than wander around with a bunch of adults in Halloween costumes."

"Cosplay," Osian muttered.

Noah's eyes drifted up and down Osian. His mouth twisted into an unpleasant sneer. "Some of us prefer to grow up. Is there anything else?"

Before either Osian or Abra had a chance to respond, Noah sauntered away from them. He disappeared into the multilevel garage. Osian dragged his fingers through his hair.

"What a prince of a man." Abra bumped her elbow against Osian. "Why don't we grab a cup of tea and consider our options?"

"Our options?"

"Noah definitely had a motive. What arrogant prick doesn't harbour a grudge when someone dumps him? I've watched all the crime shows." Abra tucked her hands into the pockets of her jacket. "How do we find out if he really was at the convention or not?"

"CCTV footage." Osian froze on the pavement. He had to speed up to catch up with Abra, who'd kept going. "What are the odds the detectives would tell us?"

"Slim to non-existent." Abra gestured toward a café down the street. "Let's get out of the drizzle. I'm not trying to catch a cold. What about Roland? Would he help?"

"Not sure a constable has access to CCTV footage." Osian waved his thanks when someone coming out of the café held the door for them. "Wait. Would the security at the location still have their copy?"

"Dunno. Probably."

"Doesn't Chris work there?"

"Oz."

"Abra has a crush." Osian didn't have space to avoid the kick to his shin. "Don't you want to say hello to Chris?"

"I hate you."

"I'll take that as a yes." Osian ignored her

complaining to step up to the counter. "We could take him a coffee and doughnut."

"Hate. Loathe. Despise you."

"Want a slice of chocolate cake?" Osian pointed to the luscious treat in the display case.

"I mildly dislike you." She grinned.

"Dannel?"

He paused in the middle of cleaning up the fire station kitchen to find their chief waiting for him. "Sir?"

"There's a detective who'd like you to chat with them about the incident over the weekend. Go on. Head out early. We'll cover for you." His chief gestured behind him. "You want someone to go with you?"

"Evie?" Dannel wanted to say no, but he couldn't encourage Osian to have a solicitor, then refuse help himself. "I need to make a call."

"What's wrong?" Wayne didn't bother with a hello when he picked up. "Did they pick Osian up again?"

"They're here at the station wanting to talk to me. Can you meet me?"

"I'm on my way." Wayne disconnected without saying goodbye.

"Rude." Dannel slid his phone into his pocket. He washed his hands, then made his way through to the locker room to get into his street clothes. Evie came in as he pulled a T-shirt over his head. "Did the chief tell you?"

"Did you call Wayne?" Evie disappeared around the corner to get changed. "I'm not complaining about getting off shift early. But I'm thinking your solicitor's a better choice than I am. He's less likely to take a swing at someone taking the piss out of you."

"Evie."

"What?" She leaned around the row of lockers to wink at him. "Just remember you asked for me."

"*Evie.*"

"Inside voice."

"I actually meant to shout that time." Dannel closed his locker and sat heavily on a bench to tie the laces of his trainers. "Why do they want to talk with me? I wasn't even in the room."

After they'd both finished changing, Dannel led the way through the station to find Detective Inspector Khan and his partner, Powell, waiting. He stared at the hand the detective held out. Evie ended up shaking it in his place.

I don't like touching people.

The detectives offered to give them a ride to the station. Dannel kept his mouth shut. He had no interest in making small talk with them until Wayne was around to deflect any mistakes he might make.

Dannel followed the detectives up the steps into the building. He paused when a man stepped out who looked strangely familiar. "Have we met?"

"No."

Dannel frowned at the oddly hard tone of the man who practically slammed into him on the way by. "What in the world?"

"Joel Brown." Evie leaned into him, keeping her voice low. "Remember? The husband of the young woman who died in the accident? Roland mentioned he keeps trying to get an investigation opened into her death."

"What sort of investigation? She died from injuries caused by an accident." Dannel watched the man trudge down the pavement out of view. "Who does he want them to go after?"

"Osian. Gemma. Abra. A few other first responders." Evie caught his shirt to pull him into the police station. "Don't worry about it. Roland said he comes in at least once a week. They have no reason to investigate."

"Why didn't he tell me?"

"Because you worry." Evie shrugged. "They've no reason to investigate. Did you honestly need the added stress? No, you didn't."

"Well, I'm stressed now." Dannel kept his gaze on the doors, watching for Wayne. "What if all the fuss brings their attention back to Ossie?"

"Not sure their attention ever actually left him."

Dannel covered his ears with his hands. "You are not helping."

Evie nudged him with her elbow. "Inside voice, Dan. Let's not draw the detectives' attention back to us."

Breathing through the sudden rush of anxiety, Dannel closed his eyes and hummed through a few bars of his favourite song. He tilted his head against the wall. Evie interrupted his attempt to find calm after a minute.

"What?"

"Wayne's here." She whistled sharply, drawing the solicitor's attention. "The detectives will be glad to get going with their questions."

"I was trying to forget."

"Better face the firing squad and get it over with." Evie pushed him off the wall. "Let's go. Detectives get grumpy when you make them wait."

"Glad you called." Wayne joined them, taking the lead. He led them down the hall past the reception toward where the two detectives were having a whispered conversation. "We're terribly sorry to keep you waiting."

"Mr Dankworth. What a surprise." Detective Inspector Powell ignored the hand he'd held out.

"Rude not to shake hands."

"Says the bloke who hates touching strangers." Evie shook her head at Dannel. "You're not helping yourself, mate."

The detectives led them deeper into the station into one of the interrogation rooms. Dannel's anxiety went up drastically. He remembered to breathe when Wayne placed a hand on his shoulders.

"We just have a few questions for you." Detective Inspector Khan took a seat across from him. He quickly set up the digital recorder in the room. "Are we ready to begin?"

The detectives asked him basic questions at first. All related to what Dannel remembered from the day of the murder. He kept his answers simple in the hopes of avoiding his mind shutting down on him.

"Do you think your boyfriend is capable of murder?" Detective Powell's query came in a lull in the conversation and caught Dannel off-guard, which had definitely been the point.

Dannel sat up straighter in his seat. He ignored the hands both Evie and Wayne placed on him, likely hoping to calm him down. "Osian dedicated his entire existence to preserving life. He'd never kill anyone."

"Maybe he blamed the victim for the loss of their patient and the end of his career?" Powell pressed him further.

"What?" Dannel clenched his jaw tightly. He couldn't stop the bitter laugh at the idea of Osian placing the blame on someone other than himself. "You—"

"Dan." Evie cut him off.

He shook his head at her. His gaze firmly focused on the empty coffee mug on the table in front of him. "He suffers from post-traumatic stress related to Ms Brown's death. Wakes up screaming from nightmares some days even now. Through every painful, gut-wrenching moment, he's never once blamed anyone but himself. No matter what I tell him, no matter how completely illogical it is. He would never have hurt Gemma. And he certainly had no motive or grudge against her. Go fish somewhere else."

"Dannel." Wayne rested a hand on his shoulder, stopping him from getting up out of the chair. "Are there any other questions, Detectives? Or have you done enough for one day? Perhaps you might want to look into the CCTV footage from the event more closely? I have it on good authority that Noah Rose was there despite your earlier statement to me that he claimed to be out of the country."

"We're aware." Detective Inspector Khan moved his attention over to the solicitor. "Maybe you should keep out of our investigation?"

"And maybe you should stop harassing my clients unnecessarily?" Wayne smiled while also managing to glare at the detective. "Haider? How long have we known each other? You're wasting your time with these two."

"Are we?" Detective Inspector Khan reached out to stop the recording after a glaring match with Wayne. "How the hell have you gotten access to the CCTV footage when we haven't gotten our full report back yet?"

"I asked nicely. You might try the technique. It's a useful one." Wayne got to his feet. He gestured for Dannel and Evie to join him. "I hope you both have a pleasant day, Detectives."

The walk out of the police station went a lot more quickly than the one into it. Wayne kept a firm grip on Dannel's and Evie's elbows, practically propelling them out of the building. He only released them when they arrived at his Range Rover parked across the street.

Dannel released a hysterical laugh and bent forward with his hands on his knees for support. "I feel faint."

"I believe they'll leave you and Osian alone for now." Warren patted him gently on the back. "You did brilliantly."

"I feel faint," Dannel repeated.

"It'll pass." Warren hunted in his pockets for his keys. "Hop in. I'll give you a lift home."

Osian got a text just as he and Abra were nearly home. "Bugger. They're on their way home."

"Why don't they meet us for supper to debrief our day?" Abra grabbed his phone to text for him. She peered over at him when he froze. "Oz?"

He stared at a man standing at the end of the street. "I...."

"Oz? What is it?" She spun around, trying to see what had spooked him. "Oh my god."

"It's him, isn't it?" Osian hadn't seen the man in months—not since the inquiry into the aftermath of the crash. "Joel Brown."

"Yes, but why is he here? And what the hell is he

glaring at you like that for?" Abra finished with his phone and handed it over. "Let's go."

"He might want to talk."

"You don't need to hear anything he has to say." She grabbed him by the hand, forcing him down the pavement in the opposite direction. "Wayne's turning around. They'll be here in a few minutes."

"Abs."

"Not happening, Oz. Sometimes, my job is to save you from yourself." Abra continued leading him far away from the spectre of his worst nightmare. "He might be a grieving husband, but it doesn't mean you have to take his vitriol."

"I deserve—"

"No, you bloody don't. We've all had patients code on us, Oz. I have. Everyone has. We can't save everyone. We're not miracle workers. You did your best, end of," she insisted. "When will you realise there was nothing you could've done?"

With a half-hearted shrug, Osian walked along beside her without responding. He didn't have an answer. It would always eat at him, no matter how illogical.

Wayne showed up in his flashy Range Rover, cutting off Abra's argument. "Fancy a lift?"

They clambered into the back, squeezing in beside

Evie. Osian reached forward to the front to squeeze Dannel's shoulder. He had no doubts the visit with the detectives had been stressful for him.

"Why don't we grab a takeaway and swing by my office? We can sit and talk over the next few steps." Wayne waited for everyone to agree before pulling into traffic. "Pizza or something less greasy?"

Letting the others decide, Osian leaned back in the seat. He closed his eyes and tried to clear his mind. It was hard to not remember the bitter hatred in Joel Brown's face.

"Ossie?"

He opened his eyes when a hand grabbed his. Dannel had twisted around in the front seat and stretched his arm back toward him. "I'm alright."

Though Dannel didn't seem to believe him, he left it alone. Osian knew they needed to talk about Joel Brown. He didn't think now was the time; some things were Dannel-only conversations.

For London traffic, the drive to the law offices went fairly quickly. Osian held back while the others trooped inside. Dannel waited with him.

"How—" Osian didn't get to finish his question. Dannel rushed him, wrapping his arms tightly around him. "You okay, love?"

"Good." Dannel squeezed him forcefully. He rested his head against Osian's. "Fine."

"Want to go home?" Osian would always put Dannel's comfort above anything else, even his curiosity at what happened at the police station. "We can easily get an Uber."

Shaking his head, Dannel stepped away from him. He grabbed Osian by the hand, though. They continued through until they found Wayne waiting in the doorway of what appeared to be a conference room.

"My office is a little small for all of us to fit." Wayne waved them inside. He shut the door and motioned for them to take one of the empty seats around the large table. "So, who wants to go first?"

Over a late lunch or early dinner, Wayne briefly recapped the conversation with the detectives for Osian and Abra. He paraphrased better than anyone else. Osian wondered if a law degree involved lessons in being concise.

"Chris sent over the full CCTV footage." Wayne wrapped up his brief speech. "Love to know how you convinced him to go through it so fast."

"Chris has a crush on Abra," Osian sang, with a grin at his best friend. She glared at him. "And Abra has one on him. It's adorable. Kind of like you and Rolly."

"Osian." Wayne glared at him.

"You are such a child." Abra kicked Osian under the table. "I asked nicely, and Chris decided to be kind."

"They exchanged numbers." Osian slipped his legs out of the way, so she kicked the chair instead. "So, here's what we know—"

"This isn't one of your podcast cases. As your solicitor and your friend, I'm telling both of you to leave this to the professionals." Wayne set his fork down. He tapped his finger against the table, practically glowering at Osian, who smiled at him. "I'm serious, Oz. The detectives have moved their attention elsewhere. Why put yourself back in their purview?"

"Purview." Osian snickered with Dannel before turning more seriously toward Wayne again. "Look, man, we appreciate your dropping everything to help us. Especially when I know you're not going to let me pay for your time—again. We'll keep our noses well away from the detectives."

"I'll pretend your deflection made me feel better." Wayne shook his head. "Have you considered Joel Brown had motive? He blamed Gemma and you in equal measure for his wife's death. Maybe he's tired of trying the legal route for revenge?"

The name hit Osian like a punch to the head as it always did. He held a hand up to stop Wayne from continuing. His breathing took several minutes to return to normal.

"Motive, maybe? But opportunity? Doubtful. We'd have seen him on the CCTV footage. I scoured every minute from the time Gemma went into the room. I never saw him. Granted, we're missing five seconds here or there when the camera turned too far in one direction or the other to see the entrance. Could someone have snuck in and out in so short of a time?" Osian grabbed the nearest bottle of water, trying to drown the lump in his throat. "And would he know how to use a defibrillator? Whoever did this knew how to override every security measure."

They had three suspects. One had the motivation but no access or knowledge. The other two had questionable motivations however they'd been at the convention and knew defibrillators intimately.

"We need to have a chat with Noah and Ethan again." Dannel shifted his chair closer to speak quietly to Osian.

"You need to allow the detectives to do their job."

Wayne spoke before Osian could respond. "I'll bring his name up to them."

"Right, of course." Osian nodded while reaching out to take Dannel's hand. "You're completely right."

"And you're going to investigate anyway." Wayne slouched into his leather chair. "Fine, fine. But I'm billing you for any hours of work directly related to you two getting yourselves in trouble."

"Sounds fair."

After cleaning up, Wayne escorted them out of the office. Abra and Evie decided to head out together. Osian got an Uber for him and Dannel to go home.

They'd had enough of an adventure for one day.

Even if Osian hadn't, Dannel certainly had. He'd been quiet the entire ride home. Osian hadn't pushed him for idle conversation.

"Want a bath?" Osian waited until they'd made it into their flat to ask. "I'll run one for you."

Dannel shrugged.

"I'll run a bath." Osian made his way down the hall into their en suite. He got the water going and sat on the edge of the tub for a second. *What an absolute shite day.* "Dannel?"

Dannel wandered into the bathroom a minute later. He'd already stripped down to his boxers. "Join me?"

"We can squash up." Osian ran his fingers through the water, making sure it was running at the right temperature. "Enjoy the warmth. The closeness."

"Ossie."

"What?" He smiled impishly at his long-time partner. "I'll even keep my hands to myself."

The next two days had been filled with work and podcasting. Dannel had convinced Osian to continue with his regular schedule. It served no purpose to take a break.

Each day Dannel found it increasingly difficult to drag himself down to the station. Firefighting had lost any spark for him. He wanted a change.

Needed a change.

He simply couldn't figure out how to make the change.

"You should talk with the Oz-man." Evie plopped down on the bench beside him. She'd already showered and changed into her street clothes. "You know he'll support whatever you want to do."

"Evie." He hushed her, glancing around the room

anxiously. "And I'm the one everyone is telling to use their inside voice?"

"You don't modulate your volume—and you asked me to remind you," she reminded him. "Besides, everyone else is still cleaning out the engine. What are you afraid of?"

"Not having a job? Being homeless? Starving?"

Evie tossed the towel in her hand toward the large basket in the corner of the room. "First, you don't have to pay rent. Your uncle isn't likely to kick you out on your arse. Second, the podcast is starting to bring in ad revenue. Third, you have friends and family who will do anything to help you. Also, maybe don't immediately jump to the worst-case scenario?"

"Podcasting isn't my dream job."

Evie twisted around to lie on her back on the bench. "What is your dream job?"

"I don't know."

"Well, maybe you should figure out what you want to do with your life? It might be good to know before you have an existential crisis about starving to death." Evie flailed when he shoved her off the bench. "Oi."

Dannel ignored her and continued lacing up his trainers. "Never quit a job before you know what you're doing next."

"Not sure it's pithy enough for a fortune cookie but

not bad." Evie hopped up to her feet. She dusted off her trousers. "Whose turn is it to mop up in here?"

"Yours?" Dannel pointed to the board on the wall, which tracked the cleaning schedule. "Pretty sure you were supposed to do it yesterday."

"Damn it."

"Have fun." Dannel got up, shut his locker, and started toward the door. He laughed when Evie grabbed the back of his shirt. "Want help?"

"I'll buy you a milkshake."

"Ortea." Their chief officer called to him from the doorway. "You've got a visitor."

"Not again." Dannel handed the mop back to Evie. "Guess I'm not helping."

"Typical," Evie muttered.

Dodging out of the way of the mop handle, Dannel grew anxious following Chief Officer Wilson. He had the distinct fear it would be the police again. Would Wayne be up this late in the evening?

They were going to wind up giving him hazard pay at this point. Or maybe Roland would take him out on a date. Wayne might prefer it to a monetary bonus.

Dannel found himself wishing it was the detectives when he found his dad waiting for him. "Myron."

"Son."

Chief Wilson rested a hand on Dannel's shoulder. "I'll leave you two alone, shall I?"

Dannel shoved his hands into his pockets and stared at his dad's chin. "To what do I owe the pleasure of two visits in a month?"

"Your mother informed me I had no one to blame but myself for the distance in our relationship." Myron sounded uneasy, though Dannel didn't really know for sure. "How do we bridge this gap?"

"Did you get some terminal illness?"

Myron stared at him for several seconds before finally laughing. "I didn't need a brush with death to reconsider my life choices."

"You sure?" Dannel shifted on his feet. He stepped back, trying to put some distance between the conversation and himself. "Ossie and I, we're a package deal. You don't like him."

"I don't."

Dannel hated dealing with intense conversations with anyone, especially family. "How do you imagine our up-and-down relationship changing if you can't be in the same room with Osian without belittling him?"

"He gives as good as he gets."

His dad did have a point. Osian had a habit of picking fights with him. Dannel had refused to get involved. Mostly because Osian was generally right.

Myron had a poor track record, after all. They'd tried so many times to meet in the middle and rebuild their relationship. Why bother?

"Why don't we head to your place? We can talk on the way. I'll do my best not to rise to Osian's prodding." Myron took a step toward him. "What's the harm in trying?"

Dannel could honestly think of a number of reasons to say no. His young heart had been shattered when his dad walked out on them. He'd come back, but the damage was done. "Why do you always want to do this after a long day of work?"

"You ignore my calls on your days off. And you never answer the door when someone knocks."

"Right." Dannel had no retort to either of those points. He did ignore people who called or showed up at the flat, particularly if Osian wasn't home. "Okay. Fine."

The walk home started out awkwardly. Dannel was tired and had nothing to say. His dad seemed hesitant to open the conversation, for someone who'd wanted to chat.

"Why did you leave?" Dannel paused at a light and found himself unable to keep the question inside.

"Son." Myron shoved his hands into the pockets of

his jacket. "Did you have to go for the gut immediately?"

"I don't understand what you mean." Dannel repeatedly punched the button to change the light. "You say you want to talk. Well? Why'd you run off?"

Myron was silent until the light changed and they'd begun to walk again. "I was young. Incredibly immature. I had a million dreams for my future. And I thought I had all the time in the world to come back and pick up my family where I'd left them. I wasn't ready to be a parent."

"And Mum was?"

He shook his head sadly. "No, she wasn't. I'm honestly amazed she ever let me talk with you or Roland ever again."

"So am I."

His brother had been thrilled to reconnect with their dad as a teenager. Dannel had required a lot more convincing. Even now, he kept Myron at arm's length.

Dannel stayed quiet all the way to his street. He paused at the sight of the figure hanging out by their flat. "What's he doing here?"

"Who?"

Dannel ignored his dad. He picked up his pace,

trying to catch Ethan by surprise. "Are you waiting for someone?"

He bolted.

Dannel watched, completely bewildered, as Ethan raced out of sight. "What the—"

"Friend of yours?"

"Used to be." Dannel didn't know what to think of Ethan anymore.

His dad, after their conversation, had decided not to push the subject. They made a tentative date to have lunch later in the week. Dannel watched him leave, then jogged up the stairs.

He found Osian standing by the window with binoculars. "What are you doing?"

"Spying on Ethan spying on me." Osian caught him by the wrist to drag him over. He looped his arm around Dannel's neck and pulled him in for a kiss. "What do you think he wanted?"

"We'll have to ask him."

"Do you honestly think Ethan's going to answer the door?" Dannel followed Osian down the street. They'd made their way once again to Gemma and Ethan's flat. "He knows I saw him last night."

"We're about to find out." Osian thought Ethan would answer if only to deflect whatever suspicions they had. "Here we go."

He knocked.

And knocked.

His confidence faded a little. Osian decided to continue ringing the bell and knocking. Ethan had to answer eventually, even if it was just to yell at them to go away.

Osian's instinct proved correct when the door was yanked open five minutes later. "Morning."

"Will you quit ringing my sodding doorbell?" Ethan looked ready to start a fight with them. "What do you want?"

"Shall we come inside? Or would you like to give the lovely people walking their dogs even more of a show?" Osian waited until Ethan moved away to allow them in. "Tea? Cakes?"

"Don't push your luck," Ethan growled. He went through to the living room, not bothering to see if they were following. "I'll throw you out on your ear."

Osian glanced back at Dannel, then to Ethan again. "I like our chances of taking you. Why don't you tell us why you were skulking around our flat last night?"

"I don't know." Ethan flopped down onto the couch.

Osian sat gingerly in one of the armchairs across from him. He'd never seen Gemma's place so grungy. There was half-eaten food on dirty plates all over. "You don't know why you were playing creepy stalker?"

"Is this sanitary?" Dannel hadn't taken a seat yet. He reached down to push an uneven stack of papers onto the floor. "I'll wash my trousers later."

"Dannel." Osian pinched the bridge of his nose, trying not to burst out laughing. He somehow managed to keep his composure. "You went to our flat for a reason."

"I'll make tea." Ethan fled the room without another word.

"Are we trusting his tea?" Dannel peered around the room. "I think something's sticking to my shoe."

"Dannel." Osian sighed deeply. He chuckled helplessly for a moment. "One, you're being dramatic. It's a little messy. He's grieving. I think we can forgive a cluttered living room. Second, no, we pretend to sip the tea."

"Is he grieving if he killed her?" Dannel whispered his question, eyes darting toward the door. "Do murderers mourn?"

Would a killer grieve their victim's death? Osian hadn't studied enough Freud to process the question, let alone answer. Then again, they hadn't decided if Ethan had committed the crime in the first place.

"Milk? Sugar?" Ethan came in with a tray with three mugs. "Help yourself."

Osian grabbed a mug and pretended to take a sip. He glanced over to find Dannel hadn't even bothered to take one. *We're going to have to work on his ability to play along.* "If you're done running out of the room to avoid us, tell me why you came over to our flat last night. Did you want to chat?"

Ethan sank down on the couch. He stared morosely into his mug before eventually glancing over at Osian. "I didn't murder Gemma. I'd never hurt anyone."

Says everyone in prison for domestic violence.

"Okay?" Osian set his mug down without taking a drink. "You were there."

"I was on the other side of the building," Ethan insisted. "We were happy. What motivation would I have had?"

"Had Gemma gotten tired of arguing?" Dannel asked.

"We weren't arguing." Ethan shot to his feet, only to flop back down with a sheepishly muttered apology. "Noah did this. I know he did."

Osian ignored his throwing the ex-boyfriend under the bus. "I'm more interested in why you haven't answered my question. Why were you outside our flat?"

"I wanted to talk."

"By running away?" Dannel asked. He exchanged a confused look with Osian. "And hovering in the shadows like a vampire?"

"I was trying to work up my courage." Ethan

reached for his mug again, taking a large gulp. "We used to be friends. I thought we were. You immediately assumed I hurt my Gemma, and you're too busy playing coppers to help me."

"How are we supposed to help you?" Osian felt like his video game had gone into difficult mode. "We haven't assumed anything."

Dannel leaned forward, and Osian held his breath, hoping he didn't show their hand too soon. "You ran off. Innocent people don't flee from their friends like they've picked their pocket."

"What?"

Osian didn't bother translating Dannel's creative analogy. "You're acting guilty of murder. If you want your friends to help, maybe let us in a little instead of bouncing between yelling, stalking, and running away from us?"

"I'm trying." Ethan set his mug down for a second time and dropped his head into his hands. "I loved Gemma. She drove me up the wall. She hated the mess I left wherever I went. And I hated her being late every moment of every day. We argued. Who doesn't? I bet you and Danny Boy fight over who gets the Play-Station controller first."

"We don't." Dannel shrugged. "I go first."

Osian rubbed his forehead, giving up on trying not to laugh. "Not what he meant, love. I leave my wet towels on the floor."

"Yes, you do. And I drape them across your side of the bed." Dannel glared at him. "You also forget to close biscuit packets. They go stale. Stale."

"Pretty sure we're proving his point," Osian admitted ruefully. He shifted his gaze from Dannel to Ethan. "How did you think we could help you?"

"Prove I'm innocent."

"We're not the police."

"And? It hasn't stopped you from investigating up to this point. I've listened to your podcast. Gemma loved them—never missed an episode." Ethan got to his feet and began to pace the room. "The police are going to arrest me."

"Did you do it?" Osian watched Ethan's face carefully to see his reaction. "Were you in the room when she died?"

"No, I sodding wasn't." Ethan had his fists clenched tightly at his side. He started toward Osian but stopped himself. "I didn't kill her."

"Ossie." Dannel stretched his foot out to nudge Osian.

"Yeah, I know." He scratched his head roughly and

sighed. "He believes you. And apparently, we're going to attempt to help you."

And me.

Even if I still think there's the tiniest chance you might be guilty.

"What do we do?" Ethan was suddenly eager to chat with them. "What do you need to know?"

Ignoring the cynical part of his mind, Osian decided Ethan's guilt or innocence didn't matter. If he answered their questions, the truth would present itself eventually. He hoped.

"What do you remember before she left with the defibrillator?" Osian went with the most obvious question first.

The police hadn't exactly been open to sharing information with them. Osian thought if they figured out who'd drawn Gemma away from the first aid station, they'd find the killer.

Whether it's Ethan, Noah, or someone else entirely.

"Someone called in an emergency. It went over the tannoy." Ethan wrapped his arms around himself. "We'd had four similar calls through the morning. All pranks. We'd gotten to the point where only one of us went. I'd handled the previous one. It took me across the building to an out-of-the-way space not being used. I didn't find anyone, so I trudged back to Gemma. She insisted on responding next."

"Did anyone identify who was playing the pranks?" Dannel shifted uncomfortably in the chair. He rested his hands gingerly on the arms of the seat. "It can't be a coincidence."

"A question for the police." Osian wondered if they could convince Detective Khan or Powell to offer any insights. "Why don't I text Abra? She might convince Chris to see if the security office looked into the calls."

"Or kill you for making her reach out to her crush." Dannel had an excellent point.

"I'll text Chris. Tell him to call her instead."

They'd intended to see Noah. Instead, they went through every detail of the day of the murder with Ethan. It took so long, Dannel was almost late for work; he barely had enough time to get home, change, and jog the short distance to the station.

Osian had watched him leave before calling Abra. "Hello, Abs."

"I hate you."

"Did Chris call? Have a date?" He grinned at the creative string of curses being shouted at him. He waited for her to pause for a breath. "Want to come over? Dannel's at the station. I'm by my lonesome trying to decide if Ethan's a murderer or simply an inept boyfriend."

"Fine. But you're buying dinner and explaining to me why you told Chris to call me," Abra grumbled. "Pizza, curry, or burgers?"

"Surprise me."

"Tofu it is."

The mood in the station set Dannel on edge immediately. Evie joined him on the way into the locker room to change. He couldn't shake the feeling all eyes were on him.

"Did I do something weird again?" Dannel whispered to Evie when she sat beside him on the bench. "Why's everyone staring at me?"

"No one is staring at you. I mean, I am, but I'm talking to you." Evie frowned at him. "It's just anxiety."

Despite her encouragement, Dannel's unease grew throughout the evening. He tried to bury the anxiety by throwing himself into a thorough clean of their fire engine. It wasn't his turn, but he didn't care.

"Ortea?"

Dannel moved around the engine to find their chief waiting for him. "Sir?"

"Let's talk." He motioned for Dannel to follow him.

Dannel's blood pressure shot up. He wiped his hands on his trousers and climbed down. "Something wrong?"

"Come up to my office."

Dannel followed Chief Wilson through the station up into the small room that was more suited to a closet than an office. He squashed himself into the fold-out chair. "Am I in trouble?"

"I'm not your headmaster."

"Sir?"

He sat on the edge of his desk. "You're not in trouble."

"But?" Dannel hated the chief's office. He rarely felt claustrophobic, and the room made his entire body itch. "Am I being fired?"

"What? No."

Dannel rubbed the palms of his hands across his knees. "Why is everyone acting strangely?"

"We want to help."

He wondered if he'd blacked out and missed an entire part of the conversation. "I am confused."

"Your boyfriend was arrested for murder." Chief

Wilson spoke quietly. He rested a hand on Dannel's shoulder. "You didn't know."

"What?" Dannel tried to catch his breath, but it seemed to stick in his throat. He counted slowly in his head, inhaling and exhaling until his vision stopped tunnelling. "Who.... When...."

He couldn't put together an actual question. Osian had been arrested. It seemed completely illogical, given his conversation with the detective.

"Abra Gidney contacted me. She was on the way to the police station with Osian's solicitor. We assumed you knew." Chief Wilson moved off his desk to crouch in front of Dannel, who'd put his head down between his knees. "Breathe, son."

"Arrested."

"Ms Gidney didn't seem concerned. But why don't you let me drive you down to the police station?" He stood up and reached down to help Dannel to his feet. "You're part of our family. We take care of our own."

They arrived at the police station to find Wayne had already ripped into the detectives. Chief Inspector Callum Banks had taken him aside for an in-depth conversation. Dannel patiently waited with his boss by the front desk.

"Patiently" was definitely a stretch.

He stalked nervously around the room, periodically asking the constable manning the desk for an update. She was gentle in her refusal each time. Her kind answer, though, remained the same.

"Dannel." Wayne came through the door to the left of the front desk after thirty agonising minutes. "Why don't you join us? You'll want to be part of this conversation."

Dannel shook his arms out, trying to stop the trembling in his hands. "Chief?"

Wilson waved him off. "Go on, son. I'll wait here for a while."

Following the solicitor, Dannel reminded himself to keep his voice measured and make eye contact with the detectives. *Don't stare. Just meet their gaze, then look away after a few seconds. You'll be fine. We'll get Ossie out of here and find the prat responsible.*

Instead of leading him to an interrogation room, Wayne brought him further into the police station. They went into a larger office. It was packed with three detectives, Chris Kirwin, Abra, and Osian.

"Ossie." Dannel found it impossible to move when he spotted Osian.

Osian stepped around the others to rush over and drag him into a crushing embrace. "I'm okay. It's okay. We're *all* going to be okay."

Conversation swirled around them. Dannel tuned

all of it out, reassuring himself Osian was truly fine. He'd had too much time to work himself up over worst-case scenarios.

"What happened?" Dannel whispered.

"The detectives received CCTV footage showing me entering the room *before* Gemma." Osian tightened his arms around him when Dannel tried to pull away. "It's obviously fake. Abra called Chris, who rushed over to help them dissect and compare both sets of video."

"So, you're not being arrested for murder?"

Osian stepped away from him. "No. I think they're more concerned now about why someone is so insistent on me being arrested for murder."

"Finally." Dannel glared over Osian's shoulder at the detectives. "What took them so long to figure out the painfully obvious?"

"*Dannel,*" Wayne muttered pointedly. "Why don't we all sit down and discuss where to go from here?"

Reluctantly releasing Osian, Dannel dropped into one of the chairs farthest from the detectives. He folded his arms across his chest. His anxiety had flowed into an irate irritation.

"They're doing their best, love." Osian nudged him in the arm. "Ease off on the glare of death."

There was an awkward silence. Dannel watched

the three detectives muttering in a huddle together by the door. He wondered who the third one was.

"We haven't been introduced. I'm Chief Inspector Callum Banks." He motioned for the other detectives to take their seats. "We apologise for the disruption our investigation has caused. We haven't been able to identify where the anonymous tip came from."

Osian leaned in to whisper to him, "Because it's anonymous?" They snickered together before Wayne cleared his throat loudly. "Sorry."

"The question we're hoping you might be able to answer is what links Gemma and Osian." Inspector Banks held a hand up when Osian went to comment. "Aside from the obvious of their all being paramedics."

"What about the accident?" Dannel asked.

"The two of us worked on a fatal accident in London over a year ago." Osian's hand tightened on Dannel. "Terrible incident. Multiple vehicles, one of which caught fire on impact. Several fatalities on scene. It wasn't just us. Abra and Archie were there along with a host of other first responders."

"Where's Archie?" Wayne asked.

Dannel turned toward Osian. "Archie? Isn't he off finding himself again?"

After the terrible London accident, Osian hadn't

been the only one to quit. Archie had trekked around the world. They'd hardly seen him in the past year.

"Archie?" Inspector Khan drew them out of their murmured chat. "Who is Archie?"

"Archibald Dennis." Osian reached out blindly to grab Dannel's hand. "Archie. We traded off partnering with Abra and Gemma, depending on what shifts we were on."

"He's climbing a mountain somewhere," Wayne added helpfully.

"How does this relate to the case?" Inspector Banks tried to draw the conversation back to their investigation. "You mentioned him for a reason."

"Setting aside your other suspects for the sake of argument, what I believe they are suggesting is that if someone targeted Gemma because of her role in their family member's death, the other paramedics involved might also be at risk." Wayne held a hand up to stop Dannel or Osian from interjecting. "I'd never want to tell an officer of the law how to handle their case. But it seems you have two avenues of motive. Either it's personal for Gemma, and either her ex or her current beau is responsible. Or there's a larger issue at hand. My clients might need protection. I sent over the information on Joel Brown to you."

"We'll look into him, of course. You didn't find him

on any CCTV cameras around the time of the incident at a cursory glance." Inspector Powell jumped into the conversation. "We'll give it a closer look."

"Have you crossed Osian off your list officially?" Dannel didn't dignify Wayne's muttered warning with a response. He wanted confirmation the detectives had officially decided Osian was innocent. "And given the faked CCTV footage, maybe you shouldn't take not seeing Joel Brown, Noah, or Ethan as a given?"

"Inside voice" was Osian's only response.

Dannel stared down at their joined hands resting on his leg. His mind kept considering the four paramedics. He sat up quickly. "Osian might be in danger."

"Of course I'm not," Osian said confidently.

Dannel wasn't so sure. He tapped his fingers anxiously against the side of the arm of his chair. "If the killer can't blame you for Gemma's murder, what's to stop them from coming after you in another way? Even if it's not Joel, someone wanted you to be arrested for murder."

Osian glanced from Dannel to the detectives. "I was really enjoying pretending not to be stressed for all of a minute. I don't need both you and Wayne reminding me of the danger."

"I could be wrong." Dannel tilted his head to stare up at the ceiling. "What do we do now?"

The detectives launched into a lengthy discussion about being aware of their surroundings. They suggested staying somewhere else. Dannel felt all his anxiety returning, but for a different cause.

He did not do well staying in someone else's home. He knew their flat. It offered him sanctuary to hide from the world.

"Or we could make sure all the tenants know to keep the front door locked and not allow guests in until the situation is resolved." Osian knew him well enough to understand his immediate tensing. "We'll manage. We can take care of ourselves."

"All the same. It wouldn't hurt to be more cautious," Inspector Khan interjected. "We don't want anyone else getting hurt. And we certainly don't know for certain who's responsible."

"Agreed." Chief Inspector Banks nodded. "If you don't want to stay elsewhere, we'd appreciate you at least taking extra precautions."

They made "extra precautions" sound like a mere inconvenience. Dannel knew better. He scrubbed his fingers roughly across his forehead.

"We're open to suggestions." Osian finally broke the silence. "Especially ones not involving us being locked up for our own safety."

T he thrill of investigating a case of their own and not simply reporting on one for his podcast faded away when reality hit. Osian and Dannel had both been a little shell-shocked. Wayne had suggested they call in reinforcements to talk things over.

In other words, Wayne hoped a cluster of their loved ones would talk some sense into them. Osian couldn't blame the solicitor, but he still disagreed on how best to handle the situation.

The killer or killers were an unknown entity. A ghost. Osian didn't see a point in attempting to protect themselves from the hint of danger. Even the police hadn't known for certain.

"So, we're not hiding." Osian started the conversation with the most important part. He and Dannel both agreed quite strongly on it. "And you know how stubborn we can be."

They'd all gathered at Roland's place. Osian hadn't wanted to worry anyone. Dannel figured their friends and family were already concerned; they might as well be stressed about the truth.

It was a fair point.

"We're definitely not hiding," Osian reiterated. He peered around the living room at those who'd been able to make it on short notice. "We're going to be a little more cautious."

"A lot more cautious." Wayne had definitely kept them from sugar-coating their meeting with the police. "I still believe you should stay somewhere other than your flat for a few days."

"I agree." Roland threw in his opinion.

Osian didn't need to glance around the room to know everyone agreed. "If the killer or killers are after me, how is staying somewhere else going to do anything other than delay the inevitable confrontation? We can't hide indoors indefinitely. Dannel has a job. We need fresh air. I'll wilt without it. I'm a sensitive house plant."

"*Oz*." Olivia threw a pillow at his head.

Of their gathered friends, only Abra and Evie

seemed to understand his point. The police had plenty of theories. No one knew for certain if the killer had intended to target their entire group—or just Gemma.

Evidence pointed in both directions, in Osian's opinion. He didn't think they should assume the killer wanted to rampage through multiple former paramedics. What if it turned out to be a jilted lover like Noah?

"Oz?" Abra followed him into the kitchen. "I tried texting Archie."

"And?"

"Nothing. No response to email. He hasn't been on Facebook in a week." Abra shifted nervously in front of him. "I called his mum. She hasn't heard from him either."

"He's climbing a mountain, right? He probably doesn't get Wi-Fi up there." Osian didn't think Archie would appreciate them panicking while he was finding his inner peace. "He goes months without seeing anyone. It's not out of the ordinary."

"Aren't you worried at all?" Abra clutched the glass in her hands tightly. "Even a little?"

"I'll worry when I have a reason to do so." Osian didn't want to admit his concerns. "Has his mum reached out to the tour company? Maybe they'll be able to make contact."

"I'll send her a text." Abra leaned against the counter. She met his gaze after a few seconds. "We did nothing wrong that day, Oz. Nothing. We did our jobs. We're not miracle workers. Bringing people back from the dead isn't within our powers."

"I know." Osian mostly believed it to be true. "Not everyone agrees, apparently."

"That is *not* your fault." Abra set her glass down and walked over to hug him. "Or mine. It wasn't Gemma's or Archie's."

Osian twisted away from her. He wandered over to stare blankly into Roland's fridge before shutting the door. "Someone out there doesn't appear to agree."

"Oz."

"Am I interrupting?" Roland joined them in the kitchen. He nudged Abra with his elbow. "Can I have a minute with the Oz-man?"

"Fine." Abra grabbed the bottle of wine off the counter and sauntered between them. "We'll be talking about you behind your backs while you're in here."

"So, Rolly, what's the story?" Osian went back to leaning against the counter. "Now that we're alone, are you going to confess your love for me?"

"First, it's Roland. Second, no, I'd rather lick a hairy toad." He gave a long-suffering sigh. "We have to talk to Dannel. He's not understanding the danger."

It was Osian's turn to sigh very deeply and for an extended length of time. He didn't want to have this conversation with Roland. Years of experience told him how a chat that started with "Dannel doesn't understand" would go.

Nine times out of ten, it wound up with Osian losing his temper.

"Danny does understand the danger." Osian thought Dannel had a better grasp of the danger than he did. "And you should definitely be having this conversation with him—not me."

Roland peered anxiously into the living room. "I love my brother."

"Then love him enough to trust he does actually understand far more than you give him credit for." Osian mimicked dropping a mic, then left Roland in the kitchen to think it over. "Might want to bring more crisps. The masses are ravenous."

The others had gathered in the living room to take their minds off the strain by playing a rousing game of Cards Against Humanity. Osian slid to the floor by the couch, sitting next to Dannel. He motioned for Evie to deal him a hand.

Roland joined them a few minutes later. He tossed

out a few bags of crisps and managed to squeeze in between his aunt and uncle. "We're only playing if everyone agrees to keep their tempers."

"As opposed to last time when you threw the cards out the third-story window of my flat?" Wayne saluted Roland with his mug of wine. "We spent thirty minutes trying to find all of them. My custom pack."

"Rolly? Is there any more wine?" Evie hefted up one of the empty bottles on the table.

"We're going to have many regrets in the morning." Roland shook his head. "And you're all sleeping over if you can't see straight."

Despite protesting about not wanting to stay elsewhere, Dannel woke up to find himself squashed up with Osian on Roland's sofa. His legs dangled over the arm of it. He grunted in pain and tried to sit up without falling off.

"Ossie?" he whispered.

Osian shifted slightly, knocking Dannel onto the carpet. "Shit. Sorry, love."

"Wine hangovers are the worst," Dannel grumbled. He stretched out on his back on the soft carpet and tried to get his back to straighten out. "Did we all crash at Rolly's?"

"Pretty sure your auntie and uncle went home." Osian leaned up on his elbow to glance around the room. "I spy with my little eye a couple canoodling in the corner."

Dannel twisted his head and spotted Abra and Chris whispering to each other over their coffee. "Don't make it awkward."

"Oi, Abs. Sleep well?"

Dannel reached up to flick Osian on the arm. "What did I say about not making things awkward?"

"The last time I had this many hungover people in my house, Chelsea had won the title." Roland stood in the living room, appearing as pained as Dannel felt. "Or was it Tottenham?"

"Do not get them started." Abra threw a pillow at Roland. "They won't stop."

As a couple, Dannel thought they agreed about everything. Their one point of contention had always been football. Tottenham versus Chelsea. It always devolved.

"But, Abs." Roland dodged out of the way of a second pillow. "I'll arrest you for assaulting a constable."

"Don't tempt her to make the arrest worthwhile. She'll kick your arse from here to the police station and back." Chris got to his feet slowly. He went over to sit on the chair across from Dannel and Osian. "When do you want me to come over to set up the security system?"

"I don't want to plug into the Matrix." Dannel knew enough to know systems could be hacked. "Aren't there any low-tech solutions?"

"Low tech?" Chris exchanged a glance with Roland over Dannel's head. "Would you settle for a camera by your front door?"

"There are CCTV cameras all around the street outside." Osian appeared to be as uneasy as Dannel about the idea of having hackable technology inside their home. "We could change our locks."

"Why don't I drive you both home? I can give you an idea of what the setup would be. It's not intrusive. No one's going to be spying on you," Chris offered. "I can't force you to make changes to your personal security, mate. Think about it? You shouldn't make decisions without all of the information. Hear me out at least. What's the harm?"

"He's trying to trick us into plugging into the system." Osian winked at Dannel, who chuckled. "Next, he'll say there is no spoon."

"If you two nerds could get a hold of yourself for a second." Chris laughed good-naturedly at them. "Why don't we go pick up breakfast and head over to your place? I'm not due into work until this afternoon."

Dannel peered up at Osian, who shrugged and nodded. "Fine. We're not agreeing to cameras in the loo."

"You're both ridiculous."

After a lot of moaning at being awake, they were ready to leave. Dannel had made sure to help Roland clean up the living room first. It hadn't seemed fair to leave him with a mess to handle all on his own.

"Danny."

He paused on the way out the door, letting Osian and Chris go first. "Rolly?"

"Why must you insist on calling me Rolly? Constable Rolly." Roland scratched his head roughly. "No one's ever going to take me seriously."

"Did you want something aside from whining?" Dannel simply stared at his brother. "Please be aware I have not consumed caffeine. And we drank wine. Lots of it. Bottles. All of your bottles, in fact."

Roland snickered with him for a second. "Be careful, yeah? You're the only brother I've got. I'm attached to you."

"Is this bonding? You suck at it." Dannel suffered through the tight hug from his brother. "Aren't the police supposed to be more stoic?"

Leaving his brother to deal with the rest of the leftover guests, Dannel jogged down the stairs to catch up with Osian and Chris. They were standing by a Range Rover while Chris and Abra said goodbye. He snuck up to wait without disrupting them.

"Aren't they adorable?" Osian whispered.

"Pretty sure you're still making everything uncomfortable for them." Dannel grinned when Abra glared at both of them before walking off. "They are sweet."

"Are you two quite finished?" Chris unlocked his vehicle. "Get in. We'll grab breakfast at Pret on the way to your flat."

They picked up breakfast at the Pret not far from the building. Chris drove a loop around their building. He pointed out the various security cameras on the shop as well as the obvious gaps in their view.

All the way up to their flat, Chris insisted on assessing their lack of security. Dannel was feeling distinctly paranoid by the time they'd gotten inside. He wanted to hide inside the bedroom and never come out.

"Chris." Osian finally snapped at their friend. "Maybe reel in the dramatics? We need to be able to sleep at night."

Chris sat at one of the chairs around their small kitchen table. "I promise the system I want to set up for you won't be intrusive. No cameras in your bedroom. I'm more interested in ensuring no one gets into the building or your flat without express permission."

"Uncle Danny's in charge of the building. He'll have to approve any changes."

Osian came up behind Dannel, resting his chin on his shoulder. "And he's not prone to spending money unless absolutely necessary."

Dannel hid his smile behind his sandwich. His uncle had no issues spending money on the building or on his nephews. "I don't want cameras in my home. Or weird things hackers can use to talk to me. I'd never sleep again."

Chris bent forward to rest his head against the table. "I'm not suggesting you invite big brother into your place, for Christ's sake. I want you to be safe. Maybe a camera on the front door of the building, inside and out. It wouldn't hurt to change your locks either."

Since neither of them could remember the last time the locks had been changed, Dannel didn't really have an argument against it. He hated having people in the flat. They disrupted his calm.

It was the main reason they'd never gotten a pet. Animals, like people, tended to make messes. They were noisy.

So much noise.

"Why don't we start with the locks?" Chris knew how to pick his battles. "I'll chat with your uncle. I can get all the inner and outer doors changed out. We'll tell the other tenants I'm simply upgrading the security. While I'm fixing those, you two chat about cameras."

Grabbing his mobile, Chris left to coordinate with his office and their uncle. They both collapsed onto the couch with tired groans. Dannel was glad the fire chief had given him a few days of vacation.

Dannel twisted around to lie on the couch with his head in Osian's lap. "I don't want cameras in the flat."

"I know."

"And I want to find who did this to Gemma."

"Me too." Osian dropped his hand down to rest on Dannel's head, massaging gently. "Why don't we go track Noah down?"

"Not sure Chris or Rolly or the detectives would consider that safe or sane behaviour." Dannel tilted his head to grin up at Osian. "How do we figure out where Noah is?"

"How do you find a self-absorbed narcissist?"

"Instagram?"

Osian trolled Instagram and unsurprisingly found Noah had documented every moment of his morning. "Will you look at this absolute wanker?"

Dannel leaned over his shoulder to glance at his phone. "He's consistent."

"Consistently a wanker." Osian snickered. "He's at the gym."

"We go to the gym." Dannel rolled his eyes.

"You go to the gym. I pretend to exercise while I watch your arse in those shorts."

"Why don't we get an Uber? If we're lucky, he'll still be there." Dannel chose to ignore the jokes.

"And if we're extremely lucky, he won't try to kill us."

"So, what's the attraction to the gym?" Osian was enjoying pretending to be on a stakeout. They'd found a table outside a café next door to the gym. "I'm not getting it. Look at them; they're jogging. In place. I can jog in Covent Garden. Get whistled at, cursed out, grab a cake and coffee, and be home safely in an hour."

Dannel snorted into his tea. "Some of us care about being our best selves."

"I care about not being surrounded by the sweat of the masses." Osian had a great view of Noah through the window. "Is it wrong to want him to trip and face plant?"

"Probably."

"How are we going to get him to answer our questions?" Osian kept a close eye on their suspect.

"How about, 'Spill your guts, worm.'"

Osian spewed tea all over the table. He coughed and choked through his laughter. "You are not allowed to play *Elder Scrolls Online* late into the night again."

"What?" Dannel mopped up the tea with a napkin. "Gross, Ossie."

"Spill your guts, worm?"

"Completely legitimate line of questions."

"It's not even a question." Osian couldn't get his laughter under control. "Can you imagine his face after being called a worm?"

"We've called him worse."

"Not to his face." Osian had always believed in keeping things professional with his fellow paramedics, even the ones he didn't like. "I think he's done running."

They waited for another twenty minutes before Noah finally made his way out of the gym. Osian whistled sharply when he went to pass their table. Dannel winced at the sound, covering his ears for a moment.

"Sorry, love," Osian whispered. He patted Dannel's knee while focusing on Noah. "What a surprise."

"I'm sure." Noah didn't appear overly pleased to see them. "I'll pretend you weren't stalking me."

With an air of annoyance, Noah flounced into the seat across from them. He dropped his gym bag on the chair beside him. His entire countenance oozed confidence.

"There's loo roll on your shoe." Osian grunted when Dannel elbowed him. "What?"

Noah glanced briefly down at his shoe, then pinched the bridge of his nose. "Grow up, Osian."

For whatever reason, Noah had always brought the worst out in Osian. The perfectly coiffed paramedic who swanned around making others pick up the slack for him. He irritated Osian.

Osian decided not to play around with small talk. None of them was interested in pretending to be friends. "Why'd you lie about being at Comic Con?"

While Osian didn't know for certain, he had a hunch the man had been there. Gemma had a way of drawing people to her. An arrogant prick like Noah would've been enraged at being dumped.

From all of their podcasts, Osian knew the dangers of jealous men. He could do a hundred shows on cases of women being murdered by their exes. Gemma would certainly not be the first.

"I didn't lie." Noah sniffed in disdain.

"Your nose does this weird thing when you lie." Osian had a much better poker face than Noah. He nudged Dannel. "See it? He did the thing with his nose again."

"I wasn't there."

"You were," Dannel insisted. His fingers tapped on the table.

"And? What if I was?" Noah suddenly changed tactics.

Osian forced himself not to pump his fists in the air. "Bit strange. You being at London Comic Con. You hate cosplay. You took the mickey every sodding time I mentioned it. So you were there to see Gemma. Why lie?"

"I don't owe you an answer."

"The police will figure out you were there." Dannel lifted his gaze up from the table for a moment. "Did she turn you down again? She probably did. Gemma had substance. You don't. Were you hacked off because she didn't appreciate your brilliance?"

Osian had been watching Noah's expression. He saw the moment his mood changed and knew from experience whatever he said next would be cruel. "Don't."

Noah's attention shifted from Dannel to Osian. "Pardon?"

"You're about to say something about Dannel. And I love Dannel. Don't make me kick your arse. We'll both get arrested." Osian was unmoved when Noah shot to his feet, snatching up his gym bag. "Did you kill her?"

"No, you—" Noah cut himself off. He jerked the bag in his hand. "Harass me again, and I'll sue for defamation."

"Is asking a question defamation?" Dannel seemed oblivious to Noah's anger. "We haven't accused you of anything. What's the definition?"

While Dannel had an existential crisis over what constituted defamation, Noah stormed off. Osian slumped into his chair and sipped the remainder of his tea. He listened absently to the muttering beside him.

"Not actually defamation." Dannel shoved his phone into Osian's face. "See?"

"Don't think he cares." Osian tilted his head back slightly. "What have we learned?"

"Noah has a temper."

"What new information do we have?" Osian clarified his question.

"Noah was at the convention."

"Exactly. And I'd wager both of our bank accounts he not only saw Gemma but argued with her." Osian didn't believe it proved his guilt or innocence. "He's definitely moved up my list of suspects."

"If it was Noah, why would he attempt to make the police think you're the killer?"

"He loathes my existence?" Osian had no doubts Noah would be thrilled to see him in prison. "And I'm an easy target. I was there."

Deciding to head home before the skies opened on them, Osian opted to hail a passing cab. They didn't want to risk the Tube or a bus. It might make Chris and Roland less likely to shout at them for leaving their flat without telling anyone.

They arrived home to find a locksmith kneeling down by their front door. Chris and Dannel's uncle were standing off to the side in conversation. Both men turned towards them when they hopped out of the cab.

"Maybe we should get back in and go for a drive?" Osian peered over his shoulder at the cabbie that had already pulled away from the kerb. "Never mind. We're on our own. Time to face the firing squad."

"Good luck." Dannel dodged by his uncle, squeezed by the locksmith, and disappeared up the stairs into the building.

"Brilliant." Osian didn't blame Dannel. He didn't handle confrontation well at all. Their brief interrogation of Noah had likely been enough for the entire week. His attention turned to the unhappy men in front of him. "Hello. Looks like rain."

"Looks like someone's got a death wish." Chris appeared completely unamused. "What happened to staying in the flat until we sorted your security?"

"I do not remember having a conversation about staying in the flat. I do recall you leaving us to decide what we wanted to do. And we opted to go for a walk." Osian figured going from a car to the café counted as exercise. "So? How goes the lock changing?"

"Oz." Chris reached out to grip his shoulder firmly. "I don't want you to get hurt."

"And we weren't."

"Osian." Uncle Danny stepped up beside Chris. "If you're not worried about yourself, what about young Dannel?"

"Young Dannel is the same age as I am. We're not exactly teenagers anymore." Osian didn't think they'd been exceptionally careless. They'd been in public spaces the entire time. "We were careful."

"You missed Detective Inspector Khan." Chris appeared to realise arguing with him would be pointless. "I promised to tell you to call him. So, call him."

"Shit. Am I getting arrested again? I'm tired of being almost locked up." He checked his mobile, only to find no messages from the detectives. "Well, are we being spanked for our adventure?"

"You wish," Chris teased. "I've got a date with Abra."

"Abra and Chris, not kissing in a tree," Osian sung. He knew Abra didn't enjoy physical intimacy. "I should check on Dannel."

Uncle Danny followed him toward the entrance. He caught Osian by the arm and gently but firmly guided him away off to the side. "Myron stopped by."

"Did he?" Osian wanted nothing more than to head upstairs and hop in the bath with Dannel. He knew this conversation would irritate him, particularly since Danny should be having it with his nephew directly. "And? He's been attempting to reconnect with his son. Plus he's been mostly decent to me for once."

"Why hasn't he spoken with any of us?"

"Well, I'm not Myron. And I'm not Dannel. If you want to know what's going on in their minds—ask them." Osian smiled his sweetest and most disarming grin. "Okay? Okay."

Leaving Danny still processing his comment, Osian headed into the building. He accepted the new set of keys the locksmith handed to him on the way by. *And I still don't know if Noah's guilty.*

"Love?" Osian slipped into their flat, locking the

door behind him. "Is it a musical silence sort of day? Am I talking to myself? I'm talking to myself."

Poking his head into the bedroom, Osian found Dannel stretched out on the mattress with his headphones on. *Musical silence it is.* He tiptoed out, carefully pulling the door shut.

He knew Dannel would be out for a good hour or two at least. The confrontation, no matter how mild, had probably stretched him to his limit. Osian grabbed his phone to text both Danny and Chris to ensure they didn't knock on the door.

Dannel needed quiet for at least an hour.

And I want at least an hour to figure out if Noah was lying to us. Who am I kidding? Of course he was.

But was he lying about being a murderer?

Dannel woke up late in the evening to find Osian stretched out beside him, doing research on his laptop. "Is time off supposed to relieve so much stress?"

Osian paused in the middle of typing. "Are we talking hot bath levels of relieved? Or the doctor sedated me relaxed?"

"The latter."

"Then I'd say Evie and I are both right. You should consider taking a step back from the fire department." Osian had always been supportive of whatever Dannel wanted to do. "If we're both running the podcast, with sponsors and advertising, we might make enough to pay the bills. What do you want to do, though? What would make you happy?"

Dannel shrugged helplessly. "I can't."

"Okay." Osian closed his laptop, setting it to the side and moving around to rest his head on Dannel's pillow. "Scale of one to ten, how stressed are you at work?"

"Thirty," Dannel answered bluntly. "It's taken me forever to recognise what I was feeling. I'm stressed. Every day. All day. I thought for the longest time I might be able to buffer myself from the constant barrage of sensory input."

When Dannel had been in his early twenties, he'd found pushing himself through sensory overload to be easy. Osian hated how he ignored the toll on his physical and mental health. Now, in his thirties, he couldn't disregard the strain any longer.

It was having a serious effect on him. Changes had to be made. And Osian would always have his back.

"Have you spoken with your chief?"

"What if he's disappointed?" Dannel had always had a massive amount of respect for his mentor.

"Chief Wilson? Disappointed in his favourite child? Not a chance."

"Ossie."

"I know you find this hard to process at times, love, but people adore you." Osian chuckled when Dannel poked him in the side. "You're lovable."

"Ossie."

"Just because you can't see it doesn't make it any less true." Osian ignored his protests. "You should talk to him. Make it less painful for everyone involved."

"What if I can't?"

"We'll practice until you feel confident about it." Osian knew he was making it sound simple. "We'll figure it out together."

A fter two days off, Dannel had come around to the idea of taking an extended leave of absence from the station. Odds were the change would be permanent. The idea of making the wrong decision terrified him.

Decisions, in general, caused him to waffle for ages. Osian occasionally had to prod him into moving. He had two modes of operation—instant and slow motion; there was no in-between.

Quitting his job was too important to make a knee-jerk reaction. Dannel had talked every angle over with Osian, his mum, and his brother. Evie had even been called in for reinforcement.

They all agreed he should do what was best for his

health. And he continued to hesitate. *What if I'm making a mistake? Is this going to screw up our lives?*

With Osian gone for the day with Abra, Dannel had the flat to himself. He'd made plans to head to the gym with Evie. She'd worked the late shift while he'd been snoozing—her words, not his.

Dannel had just poured himself a second mug of coffee when a knock sounded. He headed over to let Evie in, only to find his boss instead. "Chief?"

"Mind if I come in for a chat?"

Dannel stepped to the side, allowing the man into the flat. "Did something happen?"

"I think we're overdue a conversation." Chief Wilson peered into the mug. "Care to make a cuppa for me as well?"

"Of course." Dannel moved mechanically around the kitchen, grabbing the kettle for another cup of coffee. His mind didn't know how to adjust to the change in his plans. "Did you get lost?"

"No, I had Evie let me in. I asked her to give us a few minutes." Chief Wilson moved over to look out of the window. "Not a bad view."

"Sir?" Dannel gripped the jar of coffee in his hands. "Why are you here? Am I in trouble?"

"No, son." He turned around and leaned against the windowsill. "You're not happy."

"I'm confused." Dannel had been in a relatively good mood for most of the morning.

"At the station," Chief Wilson clarified. "You're part of our family. We've all been together for years now. I'll admit to seeing you all as my kids. And I have favourites. I've been selfishly holding on to you. You've been under immense pressure recently, but the job had gotten to be too much even before this blip on your radar. Am I wrong?"

Dannel blinked at him a few times. "No?"

Requiring a second to process, Dannel busied himself making coffee. He knew exactly how the Chief took his brew. Now if he could figure out how to disengage from the conversation without embarrassing himself.

I did not practice this in the shower enough. Bugger. Where's Ossie when I want him?

Wait.

Why is he asking me about this now?

Dannel handed his boss the mug of coffee. "Did Ossie speak with you?"

"No. Your brother stopped by the station yesterday."

Is it illegal to smother your brother for aggravating you in an attempt to help?

Probably.

Justifiable homicide?

"Did he now?" Dannel ground out. He might've been stressed out about having a chat with the chief, but he'd wanted to handle things himself. Like an adult. There were times some of his family treated him like a toddler. "And what did he say?"

"Don't get shirty with your brother, son. He meant well." Chief Wilson eyed him knowingly. "I suggested he allow you and me to discuss your future."

How kind.

Remind me not to trust Rolly with any more life-changing decisions. Ever.

Dannel had gone from anxious over to the discussion to hacked off at not being able to have it on his terms. "Did you two manage to come up with a date for my last day at the station?"

"Son."

"Just because something distresses me doesn't mean I can't handle myself." Dannel crossed his arms and forced himself to take a few breaths. He counted to ten slowly. "I don't want to leave you shorthanded at the station. I'm due back tomorrow for a shift. When should I turn in my notice?"

"Dannel." Chief Wilson set his mug down on the windowsill. "You're not being fired or forced out of a job. I wanted to talk with you in the hopes of finding a solution to the stress you're under. And for what it's worth, I had a serious chat with your brother about breaking your confidence."

"Sorry, sir." Dannel tried not to flush with embarrassment. "It's the noise. The constant dealing with people. The fluorescent lights. The overwhelming smells of our job. Everything piles on to me every day, and there's never enough time to decompress."

"Don't shut the door on us yet. We might find a way to make this work for you." He paused for a moment. "Aren't you interested in creating costumes? Evie Smith showed me photos of your work. I'd imagine there's decent money to be made with those. We could keep you on as a volunteer."

The chief hung around, updating him on the gossip around the station until Evie showed up. She sent him what Dannel thought was a sympathetic grin. He'd lost all interest in heading to the gym.

"I'm guessing you're not up for a workout." Evie hopped on the kitchen counter after the Chief had left. "Why don't we go for a walk instead?"

"A walk to find Roland so I can kick his arse?"

"You can't kick your brother's arse. He's a copper. He might arrest you. And if he and Wayne turn into a couple, he'll have a solicitor in his pocket as well." Evie grinned at him. "Let him stew on it for a few days. He'll be all nervous that you haven't called him out."

Dannel didn't see the point of playing games. "Why?"

"He'll assume the worst."

"The worst what?"

"Strategy is wasted on you. Trust me when I say you should give Roland a few days before you explain to him in small words that you're an adult and capable of quitting your job." Evie leaned forward, trying to snag the tin of biscuits from the counter. "If we're not going to the gym, do you want to track down Joel Brown?"

"Wait? What? Why?" Dannel pushed the tin closer so she didn't take a header off the counter.

"He's not going to talk to the police, since they won't investigate his wife's death. If he sees Oz-man, he'll recognise him immediately." Evie pried the lid off and grabbed a handful of bourbons. "Maybe we can convince him to answer a few questions."

"Not your worst idea."

"My ideas are amazing."

"Except the one where we filled the chief's office with packing peanuts." Dannel rescued the tin of biscuits from her grabby hands. "Ossie won't appreciate you inhaling all of his Bourbons."

"My ideas are always brilliant." Evie threw the last bit of biscuit into her mouth. "Well? Do you want to go?"

"We don't know where Joel Brown lives." Dannel replaced the tin in the right cabinet. He wanted time to process the conversation with the chief but knew Evie wouldn't easily let go of her idea. "How are we going to find him?"

"Women's intuition."

Dannel stared at her for a second. "What?"

"Joke, Danny." She hopped off the counter and brushed the crumbs off her shirt, ignoring his tutting at the mess. "He goes to the police station constantly. How hard can it be to run into him?"

"You don't think the detectives will find our hanging around strange?"

"Not if we're careful."

"Careful? My cosplay strengths don't stretch to hiding in plain sight." Dannel washed up the three mugs in the sink, setting them to the side to dry off. "Are you going to get us arrested?"

"No, I'm not going to get us arrested." Evie sounded far more confident than Dannel thought she should be. "There's a bookstore and a coffee shop across from the station. We can grab something to read, have a drink, and stake out the front for an hour or two. What else were you going to do with your day?"

"Stay inside where it's safe, warm, and not filled with homicidal wankers? Also, if the killer is Joel Brown, he'll recognise me. Osian and I are together enough he'll have seen me." He pointed out one of the larger flaws in her plan.

"I'll ask the questions."

Dannel decided nothing he said would change her mind. "Fine. Let's go."

"Why are we here again?" Abra had gotten tired of standing by the door and had dragged a chair over. "What are you hoping to find?"

"A clue."

It had taken some convincing and a little guilt-tripping, but Osian had convinced Chris to allow them into the Olympia. He wanted to see the room where Gemma had been attacked. They'd crossed the massive open atrium where the booths had all been set up and found the small room that had been set up for medical emergencies.

In truth, Osian had no idea what he hoped to find. The room had been completely cleared out. No signs remained of the convention or any of the aftermath of Gemma's death.

"Oz?"

He stood up from where he'd been staring at the floor. "What?"

"Check this out." Abra had crouched down by the frame. She had her phone out, using the light from the camera for a better view. "Bit of fabric caught on this jagged edge of the door. Part of a costume?"

Osian waited until she'd gotten a few photos before grabbing the scrap of fabric. "Detectives will probably want to see this."

"They're not going to appreciate your fingerprints all over it."

"Shit." Osian pocketed the fabric. "Maybe we'll mention we found this after we figure out what it is."

"Did you hear that?"

Osian barely had time to process her question before Abra had taken off at a run. "Abs."

Shit.

Jogging after her, Osian didn't even think to shut the door. He hoped Chris wouldn't be too ticked off at them. Abra had bolted toward the hallway across the atrium.

"Abs?" Osian had to pick up speed to catch up with her. "Are we chasing shadows?"

"Someone was watching us."

"It's London. Have you seen all the cameras? Someone's always watching."

"Don't be cute, Oz." Abra swatted him on the chest. "Saw a figure run down here. Come on. Let's see who it was."

"It was probably Chris or someone else in security." Osian reluctantly followed her through the door. They checked the rooms, including both of the loos. "There's no one."

"Does it smell funny in here?"

"It's the loo." Osian twisted around toward the door only to find it shut. "Bugger. I've a bigger problem. Someone's trapped us in here."

"Oz."

"What?"

"The smell." Abra darted back over to him. She'd pulled her shirt collar up to cover her nose. "They've mixed chemicals in the toilet. Get the door open. I'm texting Chris."

No matter how hard they shoved and pulled, the door wouldn't budge an inch. Osian's eyes began to water; he tried to breathe shallowly with his shirt as a protection.

"Chris is on his way. I'm calling for an ambulance as well." Abra barely managed to get the words out to explain their emergency between bouts of coughing.

Three minutes felt like an hour. Osian was beginning to wheeze. He practically fell out of the room when Chris yanked the door open.

"This is *not* being careful." Chris grabbed both of them by the arm, dragging them out into the atrium. "Dannel's going to kill me."

"We should probably stop throwing words like that around." Abra collapsed on her back, trying to catch her breath. "Ambulance is on the way. Think we're fine."

"You're both exhibiting all the signs of chemical exposure. Not sure *fine* comes close to describing the situation," Chris snapped at them. He pushed Osian to the floor when he tried to stand. "Stop moving around."

"Chris." Osian stopped to cough. "We're fine."

"Oh yes, keep choking while you're convincing me of your perfect health." Chris grabbed his phone when it beeped. "They're directing the paramedics."

"We're paramedics," Osian pointed out. "If you want to help, check your CCTV cameras. Someone had to block the door to keep us inside."

Despite his own assurances, Osian was worried about the tightness in his chest. He kept an eye on

Abra until the paramedics arrived. They insisted on carting both of them to the hospital for evaluation.

Dannel's going to be so worried.

On the ride to the hospital, the paramedics helped him rinse out his eyes to stop the irritation. They monitored his vitals. And mostly, they chatted with him about all the changes since he'd left the service.

They were treated for chemical exposure. Osian was grateful to Chris for getting them out of the loo as quickly as he had. He'd apparently found a mop shoved through the door handle, blocking their ability to open the door.

Definitely not an accident.

The police had been called. They'd had a hazmat team from the fire services out too, before they'd gone into the bathroom. Their initial report was someone had mixed cleaning chemicals in one of the toilets, enough to cause a serious reaction but not strong enough to kill.

Dannel arrived with Evie, Olivia, and Osian's mum and stepdad in tow. They all stopped when they found Osian and Abra on their way out of the hospital. "Ossie."

"I'm fine," Osian assured him. He allowed Dannel to wrap his arms around him in a fierce but gentle hug. "Totally fine. Bit of a sore throat. But I'm not at risk for anything else. Promise."

"How was this being careful?" Dannel murmured in his ear.

"I'm okay, love." Osian eased his arms around Dannel, holding him tightly. "Think about our mums fighting over who gets to hug you first."

"Osian Kincaid Garey."

Osian peered over Dannel's shoulder at his mum. "She's glaring at me like we broke her vase again."

"We?" Dannel reluctantly released him and stepped away. "You kicked the football. Not me."

Osian didn't get a chance to protest his innocence. His mum and stepdad rushed over, clutching him into a hug. "Mum. *Mum.* Mum. I don't think the doctors will appreciate you ruining their hard work in making sure I can breathe."

"Do you have any idea how concerned we were?" His stepdad eased away, though his mum clung to him with no signs of wanting to move. "All they told us was you'd been exposed to a hazardous gas."

"I am actually alive and whole." Osian sighed. He supposed he had no one to blame for their reaction. "I'd have texted you except they took my phone for the first hour. Didn't Chris explain what happened?"

"He was apparently busy with the police." Abra

pulled herself away from her mobile. "He assumed we'd contact our families."

Well, bugger.

His mum held on to him for a good five minutes. His stepdad eventually came up to help him. It was great until his sister decided to glom onto him.

"You absolutely silly bastard," Olivia grumbled at him. "Mum might've panicked."

"Just Mum?"

"We all might've freaked." She released him and went over to give Abra a hug. "About the both of you. What were you doing? How'd you even get exposed to chemicals?"

"Yes, about that. The police asked us not to speak about it." Osian looked pointedly at Abra, who'd definitely be the first to spill the beans. "I'm sure it was an accident."

The journey home was almost as painful as being in the hospital. His stepdad insisted on driving everyone. Osian endured a never-ending lecture from his mum about not taking care of himself.

Dannel kept shooting glances at him. He obviously didn't believe the incident had been an accident. Osian knew they'd be having a chat later in the privacy of their flat.

Two hours of parental interrogation later, Osian

regretted every aspect of his day. He finally managed to feign exhaustion to get his mum to leave. She promised to check in on him the following morning.

Brilliant.

Two doses of mum guilt in twenty-four hours.

"So?" Dannel closed the door behind his family and leaned against it. "What actually happened at the Olympia?"

Osian held a hand up to forestall the second, more difficult interrogation of his day. "I'm going to need tea and cake first."

"Shit." Dannel leapt away from the door when someone pounded on it. "If it's your mum, I'm hiding in the closet. She terrifies me."

Rolling his eyes, Osian wandered over to open the door, since Dannel had decided to pretend the knock never happened. He opened it to find their downstairs neighbour, Ian. The man shoved a plate at Osian, then flounced off with a dramatic twirl of his coat and scarf.

"Do not injure yourself again."

"Thanks?" Osian waved at Ian's back. He peered underneath the aluminium foil cover the plate. "Oh, cake."

Dannel came out of hiding to lean out of their open door. "Where'd he go?"

"Home?" Osian heard Ian's door slam shut. "I bet he heard Mum talking about it."

"Or she went around telling everyone to keep an eye on us." Dannel grabbed the plate and wandered into the kitchen with it. "I'll get the kettle going."

"You realise if she did tell everyone. Adelle and Stanley will be by eventually. They'll have a casserole." Osian slumped into one of their kitchen chairs. "They always have a casserole."

"It's sweet. Weird, but sweet."

"Tell me about your day." Osian took the spoon Dannel offered to him.

The day had started out well enough for Dannel. He and Evie had spent a few hours reading and sipping coffee across from the police station. They'd never seen Joel Brown.

Though, Evie had thought she spotted a familiar face heading into the station. She hadn't been able to remember who the woman was. They'd decided to head home when both of their phones had gone off with a text message from Chris.

While Dannel had stared at his phone in horror, Evie had corralled him into a passing cab. They made it to the hospital in record time. Neither of them was surprised that Osian's mum had practically bulldozed through anyone trying to get between her and her son.

"I've never been so profoundly relieved to see you." Dannel dragged a chair around the table to sit next to Osian, resting a hand on his knee. "Love you."

"I love you. I'll even let you have the last bite of cake."

Two days had gone by since the chemical attack. The police hadn't made any arrests. CCTV footage from the Olympia merely showed a shadowy figure with a hoodie and scarf covering their face.

According to Chris and Roland, the police had once again lost the suspect, who seemed to have an uncanny ability to evade cameras. Dannel wondered if the person had ties with law enforcement. Each day brought more questions than answers.

They'd gotten a few calls from Ethan—concerned the killer might come after him. Osian had been the one to settle him down. The police had the situation under control.

They hoped.

"Post. Actual, real post." Osian waved two envelopes in front of Dannel's face, tapping him on the forehead and forcing him to wake up. "Olivia ran by the post office to pick this up for us. Someone sent us something."

"Pretty sure this one is junk mail." Dannel plucked the first envelope out of his hand and tilted it toward the light. "Apparently, we could be a winner."

"You are a winner." Osian sat on the edge of the bed. "*Six: the Musical* tickets. Did you order these?"

Dannel tossed the junk mail to the side and snatched the theater tickets from Osian. "No. Is there a note?"

"Nothing, not even a return address." He showed the empty envelope. "Nothing but those tickets."

"Who'd send us to *Six*?"

"Podcast fan? Family? Someone who wanted to play anonymous benefactor?" Osian grabbed one of the tickets to inspect. "They seem legit. We're going to the West End to see six rocking queens singing about being Henry the VIII's ex-wives."

"Is it safe?"

"A public theatre? With masses of people? We can grab an Uber." Osian sounded far more confident than Dannel felt. "It'll be fine."

They'd been saying everything would be fine since

Gemma had died. Dannel didn't know if repeating themselves meant it was true. He wished.

"We're going to see *Six*." Dannel knew they'd both had the play on their to-see list. "Inside voice?"

"Inside voice." Osian chuckled. "Well? Are we going?"

Staring down at the ticket in his hand, Dannel didn't want to waste an opportunity. Someone, a fan hopefully, had spent money. He could already tell Osian wanted to go.

Dannel didn't know if his uneasiness came from anxiety at going to the theatre or a genuine concern over potential danger. He hated the idea of throwing away perfectly good tickets. "We'll go."

"*Yes.*"

"Inside voice," he teased when Osian shouted. "Keep your head. We're only going to see *Six*."

"Hilarious."

Despite the slight anxiety, Dannel was excited. They'd both wanted to see the musical about Henry VIII's wives. He'd listened to the album multiple times.

The rest of the day went by in a blur of excitement and dread. Neither of them was able to focus. They'd tried for most of the morning and afternoon to accomplish something for their next podcast.

"We're already a week behind." Osian dropped his

head into the table with a groan. "I don't want to use Gemma's death for a podcast."

"We're not using her death." Dannel didn't think anyone could accuse them of heartlessness for drawing attention to Gemma's murder. "It would at least explain our absence."

"I can't." Osian shifted his head to glance over at Dannel. "How do I talk about her in the past tense?"

"Maybe it'll help you? And you never know if your sharing the grieving process might be good for the listeners." Dannel pushed the notebook toward him. "Why don't you start with jotting notes about the police investigation?"

"I just can't." Osian got up from the table suddenly. "I'm going to hop in the shower to get ready."

Dannel stared after him in confusion. "Didn't you shower once already?"

Since the incident at the Olympia two days prior, Osian hadn't been himself. Dannel didn't know what to do. He was usually the one struggling to understand his emotions and deal with them. Osian had always fit into the role of guide through the world of emotions. Dannel hated seeing him so closed off. He worried.

And he didn't know what to do with worry.

His mum tended to cook when she stressed.

Dannel stared into the kitchen. He didn't see how making a mess would make anything better.

Right.

What does Ossie do when I'm off-kilter?

He turns the music on and sits with me until the world is easier to handle.

Dannel made his way into the bedroom. He heard the shower running, but Osian wasn't singing like normal. "Ossie?"

Osian sat in their tub with water pouring onto him. Crying.

Dannel quickly stripped out of his clothes. He stepped into the tub, sitting behind Osian and wrapping his arms around him. "You're going to be okay, Oz."

"If I talk about her case, it makes her death real."

Dannel clamped down on the urge to say not talking wouldn't change things. He'd learned over the years to get better about not blurting out the first thought that came to his mind. "I'm so sorry, Ossie."

Sitting in silence, Dannel waited until Osian had stopped crying. He reached out to turn off the rapidly cooling water. Grief was a strange beast that he didn't know how to combat.

"I'm okay, love." Osian grabbed one of their larger towels to wrap around both of them. "It suddenly hit me that Gemma wouldn't be manning first aid stations at any other conventions."

Grief is weird.

It's okay if I don't understand how he grieves.

Dannel kept up his internal pep talk while trying to be supportive. "Can I help?"

"You are."

He didn't see how he was helping, but arguing with Osian never worked. "We've got a couple hours before the show. Why don't we get dressed and head out? We can grab something to eat first."

"Dinner and a show?"

"Sure." Dannel hoped the evening went smoothly. He usually dealt with theatre crowds by keeping his earbuds in until right before the show. "It'll be fun."

They'd dressed up for the theatre, one of the only times either of them wore a tie. They both went for dark jeans and different-coloured waistcoats over long-sleeved shirts and ties; the closest to wearing an actual suit either of them ever got.

"Fancy enough?"

"For me or the theatre?" Osian went over to help Dannel with his tie. He adjusted the knot, then tugged him in for a kiss. "Roland suggested getting a taxi instead of walking."

"Did he?"

Osian left out that Dannel's brother had actually told them not to go at all. He was suspicious of the free tickets appearing in their mail, given everything.

"Working as a copper is bound to make him paranoid."

The gift of a night at the theatre was a beautiful thing in what had been a dismal few weeks. Osian wanted one good memory. He knew Dannel felt similarly.

They wanted one brilliant moment to brighten the misery. It didn't seem too much to ask. Besides, the theatre wasn't known to be that dangerous, and they'd be surrounded by plenty of people.

Not that being in a public venue had helped Gemma.

"Are we really taking a taxi?" Dannel peered out the window at the street below. "It's not that far to the Arts Theatre. Think the rain will hold out?"

"It's London."

"So, no, then?" He grabbed one of the umbrellas by the door. "Just in case. We don't want to show up at the theatre looking like we've been swimming in the Thames."

"We'd really be going out of our way if we jumped in the Thames then came all the way back to Covent Garden." Osian caught the umbrella tossed to him. "You're right, though. We'll walk. It'll take longer to wait for the cabbie, never mind dealing with traffic."

Walking hand in hand, they made their way first to Sartori for a slice of pizza. They only had to jog across the street to get to the theatre from there. Osian wondered if Dannel would be up for grabbing a drink at the social club. He was a supporting member of the Covent Garden Social Club. They attended plays often enough. He often enjoyed the bar in the basement of the Arts Theatre.

Six was everything Osian imagined. They enjoyed the hour and a half of stunningly beautiful musical theatre. The songs were buzzing in his ears as they made their way out with the rest of the crowd.

"Brilliant." Osian gripped Dannel's hand, leading him through groups of theatregoers nattering about the experience. "Are you up for a drink? We can grab one at the club, then run for it. Be home before the rain starts pelting down."

They grabbed a drink. Only one. Dannel had definitely been antsy to leave. Osian decided neither of them needed to finish their mildly bitter beers.

Dannel stumbled on the way up the stairs. "My head's gone strange."

With a concerned frown, Osian helped him up the last few steps. Dannel slipped to the floor with his back against the wall. He fished his phone out of his pocket to call for help.

"Is everything all right?" One of the theatre ushers rushed over to check on them.

"I'm calling for an ambulance." Osian wasn't feeling completely fine himself. He wondered absently if someone had slipped something in their drinks. The woman in front of him knelt beside Dannel; she appeared vaguely familiar. "Have we met before?"

Before Osian got an answer, the room began to spin for him. He sat down before his knees went out. The dispatcher on the other end of the line kept trying to keep his attention.

"Oz?"

Osian heard Chris's voice filtering through the haze. "What're you doing here?"

"Easy, mate." Chris crouched in front of him. "Sorry, I didn't get here in time."

"What do you mean?" Osian found his focus drifting away and missed whatever Chris muttered to him. "Dannel."

Waking up in the hospital, Osian found himself in a bed. Dannel was in another, just feet away. Their mums, Osian's stepdad, and their siblings were spread out in the room, all dozing in their chairs. He tried to keep his breathing normal to have a moment without their undivided attention.

His mouth was drier than Ian's wit. He'd never done drugs, but this felt like the aftermath of a bad trip. *Those bloody tickets. I wish we'd never seen them.*

"Osian."

He glanced over at his mum's breathless whisper of his name. It was almost like a murmured prayer. "I'm fine."

"You are *not* fine," she insisted. "You were unconscious for over a day. A day."

"Mum." Osian suddenly regretted waking up at all.

She pushed up out of her chair and came over to grip his hand tight. "What did I say about being careful? Not taking risks until the police finished their investigation."

"Going to the theatre didn't seem inherently dangerous." Osian hadn't honestly seen any harm in the free tickets. "It's not a routine. We don't go every week. We're not at the Social Club daily."

Nothing about going to the Arts Theatre seemed a risk.

"Perhaps now you'll listen to young Rolly?"

Osian grinned at the huff from Roland at the use of his hated childhood nickname. "Yeah, Constable Rolly."

"Oz." Roland started toward him, only to move over to the other bed when Dannel groaned. "Dan."

With both of them awake, their family members crowded around them. Olivia had the sense to make some room and call for the nurse. It didn't take long for the doctor to clear everyone out.

The doctor was pleased with how they'd responded to treatment. Osian had learned a little about poisons in his training. He supposed they should be grateful to be awake at all.

Osian sat up a little straighter when the detectives joined them. "Detective Khan. Detective Powell."

Detective Inspector Khan waited for the doctor to finish up. "Haider. Please. We'd like you to tell us what you remember."

"Play was good." Dannel had been fairly quiet since waking up. He glanced over at Osian, who tried to smile comfortingly. "We didn't drink even a whole glass of beer."

"The doctors are running tests. We're fairly confident you were poisoned." Detective Powell joined in the conversation. "Either the intent wasn't to kill you or our suspect isn't skilled. They also didn't plan on you leaving your drinks unfinished."

"Small mercies." Osian didn't need a doctor's report to know they'd been poisoned. He'd wager the killer had used cyanide laced with something other than the bitter beer. "Any suspects?"

"We believe the person involved is the same who trapped you at the Olympia." Detective Khan looked at the doctor before continuing. "Do you recall seeing any familiar figures?"

"Aside from Chris?" Osian hadn't recognised anyone at the club. No one had rung any alarm bells. "He showed up after we'd drunk the wine and begun to feel dizzy."

"We'll speak with him." Detective Powell made a note in her small notepad. "Your family informed us you'd received the tickets from an anonymous source."

The next hour was spent going over every detail they could remember from receiving the tickets to passing out in the lobby of the theatre. Osian noticed Dannel beginning to flag. The doctor stepped in a few minutes after to force an end to the questioning.

"Ossie?"

Osian twisted around on his side facing Dannel. "Yeah?"

"Why was Chris even there? Did you tell him about the tickets?" Dannel grabbed the cup of water the nurse had left for them on the tray between their beds. "How did he know we were in trouble?"

"I have no idea." Osian couldn't stop a trickle of suspicion filtering into him. "We'll ask him."

And I'll ask him a number of other questions as well.

"I had an idea."

"Oh?" Osian was struggling to keep his eyes open.

Their bodies obviously needed rest to fully recover. "What idea?"

"How many thousands of people were taking photos and vids the day of the convention?"

"Loads."

"Why don't we reach out to the cosplay forums? Someone has to have gotten footage during the time they believe Gemma was attacked. It might prove for certain whether Noah or Ethan or someone else entirely was there." Dannel set the cup back on the tray and lay down. "Is it normal to feel so worn out?"

"Definitely." Osian settled down on his side, trying to keep his eyes open. "We should rest."

He awoke later in the day, based on the change in light on the wall from the lone window at the end of the room. Roland had taken up a sentry spot in a chair next to Dannel. It was oddly quiet, aside from the odd beeping from the machines monitoring their vital signs.

"Rolly?" Osian kept his voice low to avoid waking Dannel. He sat up slowly, pleased to find he didn't feel quite so abysmal. "Where's my phone?"

Roland shifted his chair around to sit next to Osian's bed. "Think it's in the bag over there. They shoved all your personal belongings in there."

"Grab my phone?"

"What's the rush?" Roland gave a put-upon sigh, then stood up for a second time.

"Just want to satisfy my curiosity." Osian sent a quick text to Chris, asking him to come by the hospital. "Solve a mystery."

"Maybe you should both avoid mysteries for a while?" Roland crossed his arms over his chest, glaring at him. "How many close calls do you need to realise the danger you're both in? I'm not losing my brother because you want to play Father Brown."

"Kinky."

"*Osian*," Roland huffed, irritated at him.

"Nothing dangerous about sending a text message."

"There was nothing dangerous about going to the theatre." Roland had a point, but Osian refused to admit it. "Be more careful."

"This *was* us being careful." Osian hated to admit Roland was right. He'd had a bad feeling about the tickets. "Have the detectives said anything to you?"

"I'm a constable, Oz. I'm not even on their radar." Roland shook his head. "You should be resting. The doctors mentioned releasing both of you later this evening."

"Some good news, at least."

The doctors did end up allowing them to go home

later that afternoon. Osian had intended to have time to themselves. Their families had a different idea.

"I'd almost rather still be in the hospital." Osian hadn't expected so many to squash into their flat. He hadn't believed so many people would fit. "Is this even safe? I'm fairly confident they're exceeding the fire safety limits."

Dannel tilted his body until his head was resting against Osian's shoulder. They were on the couch, watching the chaos around them. "I dare you to tell them."

"Can I get away with hiding in the bedroom?" Osian knew Dannel was more than ready for time to himself. Neither of them had processed the events of the last few days. "Do they even know we're here?"

It was Chief Wilson who cleared their flat of well-wishers. He'd stopped by with Evie after her shift. One glance around the overcrowded room had him kindly but forcibly getting everyone to head to their own homes.

"I'm going to have a chat with Abra." Osian caught his friend before she could leave with the others. "Abs?"

"Hmm?" She pressed against the wall to allow his parents to go by.

"Have you heard from Chris?"

"Not a word. Bastard ghosted me on our date." Abra glared at him for the reminder. "Tell him not to bother calling if you see him before I do."

In what seemed like the blink of an eye, they were alone in their flat. Osian dropped onto the couch beside Dannel with a sigh. They leaned into each other.

"Has Chris responded to your text?" Dannel threaded his fingers with Osian's. "Surprised he didn't show up with everyone else."

"Not a word. Abra hasn't heard from him either. He basically ghosted her on their date the night of the play." Osian rubbed his thumb against Dannel's hand. "Detective Khan sent me a message earlier. They've been inundated by videos and photos after your post on the cosplay forum."

"Anything useful?"

"They received so many videos, he said it would take days to get through everything." Osian seemed inordinately pleased. "Maybe they'll finally make progress in figuring out who did this."

"Maybe."

Grabbing the remote, Dannel turned on the telly. They'd definitely worried enough for one day. The mindless drivel would hopefully allow both of them to rest and, more importantly, relax.

Osian reached a hand out to grab a nearby blanket to drape across both of them. "I genuinely prefer my theatre without a side of death."

"Hamilton would agree."

"Don't think he actually died in a theatre." Osian snickered at him. "That was a different ancient American."

"I'm innocent."

Dannel and Osian exchanged a glance before turning back to Ethan, who'd practically slammed into their flat. "Are you?"

"Detectives called me this morning. I can't believe you got me off." Ethan glared when Osian chuckled. "You know what I meant."

"Not really." Dannel glanced between his laughing boyfriend and their angry friend. "What did the police say?"

"They found video from one of the fans at Comic Con. It shows me away from Gemma at the time of her death." Ethan grabbed Osian into a hug. "Thank you. Thank you. Thank you."

Dannel moved around to put the sofa between him and the overexcited Ethan. "Have they found anything on Noah?"

"No idea." Ethan shrugged.

Several hours later, they got the answer when Detective Khan rang to ask them to come down to the station. He sent a car to pick them up. Dannel wanted to say it was unnecessary, but they had been poisoned at the theatre.

Poisoned.

They'd had two days of recovery. Dannel continued to struggle with processing the attack. He didn't understand why.

Why would someone want to hurt them?

Why would they want to hurt anyone?

"You could've stayed at home." Osian broke the silence in the police vehicle. "I'm sure the detectives didn't need both of us."

"I'm fine," Dannel insisted, probably too loudly. He wished for the millionth time it was easier to figure out the volume of his own words. "Inside voice?"

"Definitely." Osian reached his hand out to grab Dannel's. "Neither of us are fine. We will be. It's okay for us to not be okay, though."

"I don't understand why." He huffed in pure frustration. "Why is someone doing this?"

"We may never have an answer, love. Their reasoning might not be logical to anyone other than themselves." Osian had a point. A good one. Dannel just didn't find it helpful. "Ready for the police?"

"Is anyone?" Dannel followed Osian out of the vehicle, making sure to thank the constable who'd picked them up. They went quickly into the station to avoid the drizzly rain. "I'm becoming as familiar with this place as I am with the fire station."

They were met by one of the detectives who led them through the building into a small conference room. Dannel noticed a video playing on the large monitor on the wall. They'd obviously been going through the footage from the convention.

"We hoped you might sit through a few videos. I've put together a timeline from when we know Gemma was called until when we believe the murder occurred." Detective Inspector Khan sat in front of a laptop. "I'm interested in seeing if anyone in the crowd catches your attention."

It was the most boring movie in history. They watched the videos slowed down dramatically, because normal speed had made the faces a blur for Dannel. He had to force himself to focus.

"Wait." Osian leaned forward so far, he almost

tipped out of his chair. "Was that Noah? Wanker claimed he wasn't anywhere near Gemma."

The video clearly showed Gemma and Noah. They were just visible on the bottom left corner of the screen, almost hidden behind a group of Avengers. The two appeared to be having an argument from their animated gesturing.

"It, unfortunately, doesn't prove he was in the room," Detective Inspector Powell pointed out. "Take note of what he's wearing. I'll see if I can track his progress through our collection of footage."

"She looks so familiar." Osian had continued watching the video as it progressed and Noah and Gemma appeared to go in separate directions. He paused the image and moved up closer to the screen. "I know her."

Dannel joined him by the monitor. He stared at the slightly pixelated face. "I don't recognise her. She's not one of our cosplay group. Maybe you helped her as a paramedic?"

"Maybe." Osian didn't sound convinced.

They spent another hour watching and rewatching video clips. Dannel had a feeling they'd be replaying in his sleep whenever he closed his eyes. From what they had available, they weren't able to determine who'd entered the room with Gemma.

"We'll reach out to the community again. I'm sure there's more than this," Osian promised. "They all want to help any way they can. Gemma meant a lot to them."

"Home?" Dannel had been slowly shutting down. He'd pushed so far outside of his usual comfort zone for the last few weeks. His usual buffer zone had been eroded away entirely. "Let's go home."

Osian got to his feet immediately. "We'll let you know if we hear about any additional footage."

The detectives were surprisingly understanding. They didn't try to force them to stay longer. Dannel had his earbuds in and the *Hamilton* soundtrack playing before he and Osian had even stepped out of the building.

Yet another constable appeared to give them a lift home, despite their protests. The police obviously considered the threat to their lives to be real. He did appreciate the thought.

When they arrived at their building, Dannel fled inside up to their bedroom. He slipped under the duvet. With the volume turned up, he managed to slowly bleed off the stress to the strains of his favourite soundtrack.

"Fancy dinner?" Osian poked his head into the room a few hours later. "Ian brought over half a pizza.

206 | DAHLIA DONOVAN

They apparently got his order wrong and gave him a second one for free. Evie had some, and we get the rest."

"Sure." Dannel didn't move from underneath the blanket. He did ease his earbuds out. "What kind of pizza?"

"No idea. It's free. It's pizza."

"Your favourite kind." Dannel chuckled wryly. "Pizza it is. Any word about Noah?"

"Doubt we're the first ones the detectives will call. We could always—"

"Ossie."

"Yes, love?" Osian smiled sweetly at him.

"Not sure we should stick our noses in any further." Dannel hadn't been able to shake the fear from waking up in the hospital. It made him angry. "Then again, I want to stop whoever is doing this."

Anger always made him brave. Noah might be more willing to answer questions, given they'd seen him arguing with Gemma. Dannel supposed he could've lied to avoid seeming suspicious.

Lying only served to make him more suspicious, not less. Dannel wondered if Noah was capable of murder. The former couple had definitely been arguing, but did that mean he'd committed the crime?

"Pizza first." Osian flopped onto the bed, draping himself across Dannel's legs. "We'll scarf down dinner and track down the glamour model when we're done."

Pulling Dannel out of his quiet zone always worried Osian. He preferred to leave him in his musical silence as long as possible. He didn't want Dannel to forget to eat, though.

Dannel was not ready to go outside again. He needed more than a few hours of downtime to decompress completely. Osian knew his shutdown tells well enough by now.

He watched Dannel through their late supper. They finished up the remains of the pizza easily enough. He thought maybe they should put off going out until the morning.

"Don't say it." Dannel set his bottle of beer down by his empty plate. "You should go."

"What's the rush? We can track Noah down

tomorrow. We know how to find him." Osian had no doubts the man would post his whereabouts on Instagram as he'd done before. "It's after midnight. I'm going to hazard a guess the detectives won't appreciate us running out into the night to investigate on our own."

"Fine."

Osian didn't take the curt word to heart. He could see the way Dannel's shoulders dropped with relief. "Do you want to watch something on the telly, or maybe another evening of listening to playlists?"

Dannel shrugged.

Music it is.

Opting for their carefully curated video game soundtrack playlist, Osian left Dannel to make himself comfortable. He cleaned up the kitchen. His mind drifted to the woman in the video.

She'd seemed so familiar. He couldn't place her. And of the two of them, he definitely did better at recognising people.

With Dannel hidden under his weighted blanket, Osian decided to check their podcast email. He was disheartened but not surprised to find yet another threatening message. Why couldn't they leave him alone?

He considered sending the messages to the detectives. *It's probably just another internet troll. People can be such wankers.*

Would the detectives even take it seriously? Osian wondered if the emails were connected to everything that happened. *Maybe I should send them over then. What's the worst they can say?*

Moving the new email into a folder, Osian cleared out the rest of his inbox. He'd already made notes for their next podcast. They didn't want to get too far behind in their schedule.

He could make decisions about the stalker emails tomorrow. Maybe the answer would come to him while he slept. Stranger things had happened, especially lately.

"Ossie?"

Osian glanced up from the script he'd been writing on his laptop to find Dannel had emerged from hiding. "You okay?"

"Did you hear that?"

"Hear what?" Osian had been so focused on putting together the podcast, he'd tuned everything out.

Dannel shook his head, moving quickly over to the window. He lifted it and leaned out. "Oi. What're you doing?"

Osian grabbed his mobile from the table and

rushed over to peer outside. He spotted a man throwing something at their building. "I'm calling the police."

Broken glass, dripping paint, and splattered eggs greeted Osian when he got downstairs. Several windows had already been broken. The man was winding up for another throw when he caught up to him.

Osian managed to grab his arm before another window was broken. "What do you think you're doing?"

They struggled briefly over the brick. Osian managed to get it away from him. The hood fell away from the man's face, revealing Joel Brown.

The fight ended quickly once Dannel joined them. He managed to pin Joel to the ground. Osian sat back on his heels to catch his breath.

"Will you stop wiggling around?" Dannel grumbled. He glanced over at Osian. "Stanley and Ian both called the police. Evie's called my uncle. He's going to have to get someone out to fix the windows."

"What the devil were you thinking?" Osian bent forward toward Joel's head. "Why are you tossing bricks through our windows? What's it going to solve? You're just going to get yourself arrested, you numpty."

Several constables responded to the multiple calls

made. Osian wasn't surprised when Detective Inspector Khan showed up not long after. He immediately went over to speak with Joel Brown, who now sat in the back seat of a police vehicle.

Osian stood beside Dannel with an arm around his back. "What an absolute mess. Your uncle's going to be furious."

"Not our fault."

Osian stared at the husband of the woman who'd died under his watch. He appeared an almost tragic figure. "I suppose not."

No matter how hard Osian tried, that day always came back to haunt him in some way or another. It was like an out-of-control train that kept picking up speed.

"Was anyone hurt?" Detective Inspector Khan stepped over to them after the car with Joel eased away from the kerb. "Do you need to be checked out by paramedics?"

"We're fine." Osian peered around at the trashed front of their building. "Our place? Not so much. Uncle Danny's going to be so hacked off about this."

"DI Powell and I will be sitting down with Joel Brown. We've got a few questions for him about this incident and the murder investigation as well." Detective Inspector Khan nodded at them both. "I'll reach out if we learn anything or make any charges aside from the obvious for vandalism."

It was only after the detective had gotten into his car and driven off that Osian remembered the emails from the stalker. He scrubbed his face tiredly with his fingers. The messages would have to wait.

"Fancy cleaning up?" Evie held up several brooms. "Borrowed these from Adelle."

Osian took the broom she handed to him. "Who needs three—"

"Don't ask." Evie cut him off. "Dan? Be a love and grab the rubbish bin from around the corner? We can sweep up the glass into it. Not sure how we're going to get all this paint off. Might have to wait until morning."

"I'm more worried about the broken shop windows." Osian rested his arms on the top of the broom handle. "This is going to take forever. How does one bloke cause such destruction?"

"Be glad it was only one. Remember the rioting?" Evie nudged him with her broom, getting him back to sweeping up. "I don't think we slept for three days, going out to one fire call after the other."

When Dannel's uncle and auntie arrived, they joined in the cleaning up team. They'd brought

Roland with them. It didn't take much to get the glass cleared up.

The paint would require a different solution. Roland suggested renting a power washer and using water mixed with bicarbonate of soda. It should work to clear the paint off the pavement at the least.

While Roland and his dad figured out the rental, the rest of them used a water hose, buckets, and mops to handle the broken eggs. Osian knew the last thing they wanted was cemented egg yolk sticking up and becoming more difficult than paint to remove. They were all exhausted.

By two in the morning, they decided to call it a night and start over after resting. Osian slept restlessly. He was up with the sun, heading out to find Roland and Dannel's uncle already at work.

Stanley and Adelle had gone out for their usual morning walk. They'd had the foresight to pick up pastries and coffees for everyone. Osian could've kissed their feet.

Nothing seemed quite so awful with a sweet, gooey pastry to nosh on. He sat on the kerb with Dannel, who'd joined them, and pretended they were on the worst picnic in history. Or maybe it was the least romantic date, with family and neighbours joining them.

"We've had breakfast in stranger places." Dannel snagged a second pastry when Evie passed the box around. "And we've definitely stayed up for weirder reasons."

"I find none of that comforting," Adelle interjected into the conversation. "What are you young people up to these days?"

Osian winked at Dannel, who rolled his eyes. "Sweeping glass off the street. Dangerous business."

"You behave yourself." Adelle shot the three of them a stern look before laughing cheerfully. "Be sure to finish up the pastries."

Dannel had become a firefighter for two reasons. First, he wanted to follow in his father's footsteps and make him proud. Second, more importantly, he'd longed to help people —to make a difference in their lives.

Being unable to help Osian through his guilt and depression over the last year or so had hurt Dannel. He'd been pleased when the podcast rejuvenated Osian. And it bothered him that all of the progress might be stolen away by one angry man.

To distract himself, Dannel had left Osian upstairs catching up on sleep after their night of unrest. He'd helped his uncle finish cleaning up. The window repairman had shown up as they cleared off the last of the paint.

"Your handsome face will be horribly wrinkled if you continue frowning so dramatically." Ian strolled over to stand beside Dannel. "I see they've rushed the repairs. Good. I'm not fond of the plebeian appearance boarded windows give."

"Hello, Ian." Dannel kept his gaze focused on the contractors. "Wrinkles happen to everyone. You've got them. I'm going to have them."

Ian shuddered violently and made a sign of the cross. "What a terrible thing to say."

Dannel peered over at Ian, trying to decide if he was joking or not. He waited until the older man laughed before chuckling as well. "Are you off to the theatre this morning?"

"I have a coffee date." Ian smiled. "And I'm off. I wouldn't want to be anything but bordering on fashionably late."

Osian slipped out the front door just as Ian sauntered off with a jaunty wave at both of them. "He's all dressed up."

"He's got a date." Dannel gratefully accepted the mug of tea Osian offered to him. "Windows are almost all up."

"I see." Osian held up his phone, waving it at Dannel. "Noah's apparently going to be at the paramedic panel this morning."

"Ossie." Dannel was beginning to think their investigation had only put them into more danger. "Maybe we should wait for the detectives to approach him? They'll have a better chance of getting him to cooperate than we will by stalking him across the city."

Osian watched Dannel for a second and then shrugged. "Okay. How about we head down to the police station? I know the detectives received additional video footage from Comic Con. We can go through it to see if we find Noah."

Dannel knew Osian had reached the point where he had to be proactive. "How are we getting there?"

"Rolly's giving us a lift."

"You already called my brother?" Dannel blew on his tea to cool it further. He wanted to finish it up before Roland showed up. His brother got tetchy if anyone tried to eat or drink in his vehicle. "Of course you did. You probably knew I'd say no to hunting Noah down."

"It was a safe bet. But you might've surprised me." Osian threw his arm around Dannel's shoulders. "Let's get these mugs upstairs. Rolly hates being made to wait."

"He's on shift. And you hate waiting as well."

"We're all impatient prats." Osian made an excellent point while they trudged up the stairs to their flat. His phone beeped a second later. "Rolly's here."

They dumped their mugs into the sink and rushed out of the flat. Dannel made sure their door was locked. He double-checked three times, until Osian clambered back up the stairs to drag him away.

"It's locked."

"But—"

"I watched you close the door, love." Osian continued down the stairs with him. "I promise it's locked."

"Are you sure?"

"Yes." Osian squeezed his hand and gently pulled Dannel along with him out of their flat. "I am a hundred per cent confident."

Silencing the what-ifs in his head, Dannel allowed himself to be led over to Roland's vehicle. They slipped into the back seat, teasing his brother about being their chauffeur. He wasn't impressed.

"Can you two try not to get yourselves killed? Do you know how many times Mum's called me to badger me about taking care of my brother?" Roland deftly drove his patrol vehicle through traffic. "She worries. And her concern leads to me being pestered constantly."

Osian nudged Dannel with his elbow. "Is your

baby brother whining again? Did we interrupt a date with Wayne perhaps?"

Dannel rested his head against the seat and ignored both his brother and his boyfriend. "Are you *sure* I locked the door?"

"Maybe we should've gotten the electronic locks so you could check on your phone." Osian sighed. "The flat's going to be fine. It's always okay when you're stressed. If you like, why don't I text Evie to ask her to check for sure? She should still be home."

"No, it's fine."

"I'll text her." Osian already had his phone out. "Plus, she can make sure your uncle Danny's double-checked the contractor's work."

The detectives seemed pleased to see them. Dannel was distracted by a woman in a hoodie hanging out by the receptionist's desk. He pointed her out to Osian, but she'd disappeared.

The constable at the desk hadn't caught the woman's name. She'd been asking about Joel Brown, a fact even the detectives found to be out of the ordinary; Haider Khan made sure he'd be notified if she showed up again.

The detectives set them up once again in the same room. They even brought coffees and stale biscuits. Dannel chose to ignore the latter.

After two hours of scanning through cell phone footage, Dannel didn't think he'd ever recognise anyone ever again. Faces had all begun to blur together into an unidentifiable mess. He rested his head against the table with a groan.

"Why don't you take a break?"

Dannel grunted in response.

"I'll take that as a yes." Osian chuckled. He reached out to massage Dannel's head. "Why don't you head home to rest? I can finish the last however many videos there are."

"Millions."

"Inside voice. The detectives might come back." Osian continued to gently massage his head. "I doubt it's millions."

Dannel sighed. He tilted his head to the side to glance at Osian. "I'm going to be useless. I can't pick out faces anymore. Not sure I'd even recognise you in the crowd."

"Why don't you take a walk? I'll finish up, and we can head out." Osian returned to scanning through the footage on the laptop. "Wait. Is that Chris?"

He sat up to lean closer to the screen. "Maybe? Who's he talking to?"

"Someone in a hoodie."

"Describes half the people in London." Dannel sat up again. "We need to talk to Chris."

"Maybe if we surprise him at work? He's not answering my calls." Osian grabbed his mug and chugged down the last of his cold coffee. "Why don't we see if we can track him down?"

"I doubt the security office will simply let us talk to him." He wondered why Chris had suddenly disappeared on them. He didn't want to think the worst of their friend. "Maybe you should take Abra instead of me? She might convince him to talk more easily than we would alone."

"Not sure a hostile interrogation would help."

Dannel shook his head. "It's worth a shot, right?"

"Probably." Osian went back to the computer. "We've got three more videos. Why don't we scan through them quickly and then see if Abra wants to go out with us?"

They were on the last one when they found yet another piece of the puzzle. At the time the detectives believed Gemma had been attacked, Noah was storming out of the Olympia. Osian seemed as surprised as Dannel.

"I was so convinced the smarmy prat did it."

"That's what we get for judging a book by its cover."

"Smarmy book," Osian grumbled.

The detectives were happy to have proof of Noah's innocence. Yet another suspect off their list freed up time to focus on the others. They didn't seem as suspicious of Chris's presence as Dannel and Osian were.

Detective Inspector Khan tried to deter them from reaching out to Chris. "I'd prefer it if you allow us to follow up on our leads without your interference. Why don't we have Constable Ortea give you a lift home? I believe he's almost at the end of his shift."

Dannel stared at the detective inspector, who walked off down the hall. He tried not to take the dismissal personally, glancing over at Osian. "Right. Are we going to visit Chris?"

"Of course we sodding are." Osian crossed his arms over his chest. "We're not children. We've helped them with their case."

"They can sod off. We're going to chase Chris down."

"You've changed your tune," Osian teased.

"He sounded so much like Mum when she's trying to convince me not to do something. As though I'm incapable of taking care of myself." Dannel had always held a little resentment for his mum's overprotectiveness. She hadn't behaved that way with Roland. *I'm as capable as Roland.* "How are we avoiding Rolly? He's not going to take us to the Olympia to see if Chris is at work."

"We could bribe him into it." Osian grabbed his hand while they walked toward the exit. "Maybe."

Dannel had zero confidence in their ability to talk his brother around. "Yeah, not a chance. My baby brother won't change his mind for anything."

"Well, how about we avoid the problem all together? I'll text Abra to meet at our place. Rolly takes us home. We wait for him to leave, then we grab an Uber to hunt down Chris." Osian kept his voice low when they walked by the front desk. "I am a genius."

"You're something."

"Are we certain this is a good idea?" Abra fished another chip out of her packet. She'd brought a late lunch for all of them. They'd decided to wait an hour or two before heading out in case Roland decided to check on them. "Chris has made it obvious he's not interested in talking with any of us."

"He's our friend." Dannel struggled to believe Chris had done anything truly awful. "We should wait until we have the entire story."

"Hard to do when he won't talk to us." Osian dragged one of his chips through ketchup. "He might be the key to solving this mystery."

"He might be the killer," Abra stated bluntly. "You

can't pretend it's not a possibility. He's been there right after all the bad things."

"Bad things." Osian lifted his fingers to make quotation marks. "Sounds like a *Doctor Who* episode title."

"Nerd." Abra flicked a chunk of food at him. "Why don't you see about getting us a ride?"

Leaving Abra and Dannel to clean up, Osian focused his attention on pulling the right app up on his phone. They'd have about fifteen minutes. He wondered if perhaps they should take the detective's advice, but his curiosity was too strong to ignore.

"Do we even know if he's working?" Dannel's question came in the middle of their ride to the main office for the security company. "He might be at a stadium or another location."

"He's at the head office. He's there half the week." Abra met their curious looks blandly. "What?"

"I thought you'd moved on from your crush already?" Osian swallowed down his laugh. He had a feeling Abra had Chris's schedule memorised. "I'm more worried about what happens if he refuses to speak to us."

"We can't force him." Dannel had his earbuds in to dampen the sounds around them. "Pretty sure torture's illegal."

"Also, we don't know how to torture someone," Abra pointed out. She grinned when their driver gave them a worried glance. "We're joking."

Osian leaned closer to her and lowered his voice. "You could use your wily ways."

Abra pinched his ear to force him away. "We'll threaten him with your karaoke skills."

"Rude."

Their driver seemed overly thrilled to be rid of them. Osian decided they'd hunt down a regular cab for the return trip. They'd wind up being banned from the Uber app at this rate.

"Well? What now?" Abra broke the silence that had fallen after they'd all climbed out of the car. "Are we going to stand here all afternoon? I'm sure Chris will eventually find us."

Shaking his head, Osian strode forward, leaving the other two to follow him. He reminded himself they had nothing to fear. Chris had made his career helping people—not trying to hurt them.

Unless he's actually the killer and we've all been fooled.

Too late to be cautious now, isn't it?

He was reaching for the handle for the door when it swung open to reveal three people on their way out. "Chris."

Chris froze mid-conversation with one of his co-workers. "Oz."

While Chris stared blankly at the three of them, his colleagues seemed equally curious. They nudged him a few times for an introduction. Chris rushed through one before telling them to head out without him.

"What are you doing here?" Chris, Osian noticed, was studiously avoiding Abra. "I'm busy."

"Busy? Really?" Abra snapped at him. "Is that why you bailed on our date without even the courtesy of a text?"

Chris dragged his fingers roughly through his hair. He answered without turning in her direction. "I am sorry. I— Things got out of my control. I never intended to hurt you."

Abra elbowed Osian in the side. "Changed my mind about the interrogation."

"What are you talking about? What interrogation?" Chris stepped forward, allowing the door to close behind him. "Why don't we grab coffees at the Starbucks across the street? I haven't eaten yet."

"Can I make him eat my fist?"

"Abs." Osian looped an arm around her shoulder. "Practice forgiveness."

"Practice it yourself."

"We'll go down the street to grab sausage rolls." Dannel caught Abra by the arm to lead away. "You do the interrogation bit."

Chris watched them go before turning to Osian. "What interrogation? Why are you all tracking me down at work?"

"Maybe if you responded to text messages or calls." Osian had to walk quickly to catch up to Chris when he began to move away from the building. "And I can't believe you ghosted Abra."

"I didn't have a choice."

"Care to explain? How do you have no choice to stand someone up?" Osian knew he had other questions. Abra's slightly dented heart mattered more to him. "Not sure you understand how much she liked you."

"Liked?"

"You stood her up, you wanker. Not sure she'll give you a second chance." Osian forced himself to take a depth breath. "Who were you talking to the day Gemma was murdered?"

Chris paused, twisting around to glare at him. "I worked security that day. I spoke to probably close to a hundred people. Want to be more specific?"

"Someone in a hoodie."

"Someone in a hoodie? Out of thousands of people? Do you know how many of them were probably wearing one?" Chris made an excellent point. "Why are you even asking me?"

"The detectives asked us to go through all of the videos they've received from the Comic Con attendees. We happened to notice you speaking with someone in a hoodie. It's not the first time we've come across a hooded figure." Osian realised how much of a reach their suspicious might sound without the scope of everything. "You manage to show up at exactly the right moments whenever we're in danger."

"Most people would say thank you." Chris shoved Osian in the shoulder. "And you're—are you actually accusing me of being part of Gemma's murder?"

"Chris."

"I can't deal with you right now." Chris jogged away from him, leaving Osian staring after him.

Well, that went well.

I didn't even get any real answers from him.

Osian turned around to head in the direction Dannel and Abra had gone. He found them sitting outside of Greggs. "Did you get me some?"

Dannel held up a paper sack. "Where's Chris?"

"Either I hurt his feelings with my questions or he

took off to avoid answering them. Or maybe both?" Osian sank down on the bench next to Dannel. He had a large bite of the sausage roll, brushing off the flaky pastry pieces from his shirt. "What now?"

"Isn't it strange he ran off when you asked questions?" Abra bit angrily into her roll. She definitely hadn't forgiven him for standing her up yet. "He couldn't even look at me."

"Maybe he feels awful about it?"

"I certainly do," she retorted. "I need to head home. Want to share a cab with me?"

With more questions than answers, they returned to their flat. Osian hoped to sneak in without anyone realising they'd gone anywhere. He stepped out of the cab and immediately noticed a figure standing in an alley across the street.

Not again.

I'm seeing evil around every corner.

"Hello, darlings." Ian poked his head out of his flat to greet them. "You had a food delivery earlier. Were you expecting one?"

"Food delivery?" Osian exchanged a worried glance with Dannel. "When was this?"

"Oh, thirty minutes or so ago. I can't be bothered to keep time, dear. They came from Nandos, I believe. You weren't here, so I accepted it for you." Ian rested a hand on his chest. "I couldn't resist, so I may have eaten a piece or four."

"Ian."

"I am sorry." He pulled a handkerchief from his blazer pocket to dab his forehead. "I saved the rest for you. In fact, why don't you take it with you? The smells are turning me off."

"Ian." Osian darted forward to catch him by the arm when he wavered on his feet. "Dannel."

"Already dialling the number." Dannel had his phone to his ear, giving their address and explaining to the dispatcher they had a potential poison case. "I'll ask them to notify Detective Inspector Khan or Powell, as well. This has to be connected."

"I'm just hoping he's not going to pay the price for us." Osian walked Ian into his flat and got him to sit on the couch. He leaned him back against a cushion. "You're going to be all right. I promise."

"Never imagined I'd be playing out the full extent of Romeo this far into my youth." Ian's fingers gripped weakly at Osian's arm. "You are both delightfully handsome rescuers."

"Ian?" Osian shifted closer when the man's eyes drifted shut. "Tell them to *hurry* up, Dannel."

"I am." Dannel had his phone clutched tightly in

his hand. He rushed out the door. "Grabbing Evie. She should have her kit with her."

"Make sure the door's open."

"Stanley's waiting out front for the ambulance," Dannel shouted over his shoulder on his way out of the flat.

"Just keep breathing, Ian. Keep breathing."

When the paramedics arrived, Dannel went in the back of the ambulance with them. They hadn't wanted Ian to go alone. Osian had remained behind to fill in the detectives.

In retrospect, Dannel wondered if maybe they should've switched places. Osian might've done better at the hospital. He had more medical knowledge, at least.

"What were you thinking?"

Dannel frowned at his brother, who was rushing down the hospital corridor toward him. "I'm currently thinking you need to lower your voice before the nurses come after you."

"You two were supposed to stay home."

"How about you focus on Ian?" Dannel ignored his brother's dramatics. "Did the detectives take the left-over Nandos?"

"They do know how to do their job."

"Don't be shirty because you're aggravated with me, Rolly." Dannel focused his attention on the doctor who'd come out from behind the curtain where Ian was being checked out. "Is he okay?"

Since they weren't family, the doctor gave them limited information. They'd purged Ian's stomach. He was going to be okay.

With Dannel's uncle and auntie arriving, he decided to leave Ian in their capable hands. They'd do better arguing with the nurses, since Ian had no family to speak of. He convinced his brother to give him a lift home, where Osian had stayed to help the detectives.

Crime scene tape covered Ian's door. Dannel hoped they were allowed to remove it before he came home from the hospital. He could only imagine how hideous Ian would consider that specific shade of yellow.

"Ossie?" Dannel entered their flat to find Osian seated on the sofa with his head in his hands. "Ian's going to be fine."

"Is he?" Osian shot off the sofa. He rushed over to

throw his arms around Dannel. "Detective Inspector Powell claimed they had tracked down the person who brought the food. She wouldn't give us any further information aside from saying they believed the suspect used a food delivery service."

"Clever." Dannel rested his cheek against Osian's. "Too clever. Were they trying to kill us or make us sick?"

"I doubt the detectives will tell us." Osian eased away from Dannel. "I'm not sure I want to know."

"If we don't know, we'll assume the worst."

"Let's focus on the good news. Ian's going to be fine. He'll be insufferable while he recovers." Osian tried to insert some humour into the situation. "We'll have to go out of our way to soothe his nerves."

"Why don't we distract ourselves by finishing up work on the next podcast?" Dannel knew the best way to take Osian's mind off an issue was researching an episode. "Did you figure out what crimes to cover?"

After making a few sandwiches and brewing a pot of tea, they sat at their kitchen table. Osian had jotted down a top-ten list of crimes of the week. They preferred highlighting recent cases in the hopes of finding witnesses to help the police investigation.

"Why don't we do the top ten on Friday? And then we can do our own case on Monday?" Dannel firmly believed their audience would find their personal murder mystery fascinating. People tended to be more morbid than they wanted to admit. "Do we have any requests in the inbox?"

"I've been afraid to check." Osian grabbed his laptop to drag it closer. "What if we get another stalker message?"

"We call the detectives." Dannel knew they'd reached a point where they had to take the threatening emails seriously. "We should've already contacted them."

"Probably." Osian typed in the password and sighed a few seconds later. "We've got another one. And this proves they're definitely connected in some way."

Dannel shifted his chair closer to Osian to read the email. He saw the subject line. "Nandon't? I usually appreciate a good pun. Not so much this one."

"I'm texting Haider. He gave me his personal number." Osian grabbed his phone from the table. "Damn."

"What?"

"Joel Brown was released a few hours ago. They couldn't hold him without arresting him, and there was insufficient evidence. Haider was already on his way over to warn us." Osian tossed his phone onto the table. "Wonder if he'd let us interview him for the podcast?"

"Ossie."

"No harm in asking is there?" Osian made a note at the top of the page. "We'll ask him later. Maybe Detective Inspector Powell would be interested as well."

"Doubtful." Dannel shook his head at the mess they'd made of the table. "If we're having guests, we should straighten up our mess."

"They go to crime scenes for a living. Pretty sure our table covered with notebooks, pens, and laptops isn't going to shock them." Osian dutifully gathered up everything. He stacked the notebooks carefully. "How are you doing? Do you need musical silence?"

"I'm fine." Dannel waved off his concern. He'd definitely want time to decompress later when they weren't expecting the detectives. "Rolly's going to be pissed we didn't tell him about all the emails."

"Rolly's permanently annoyed with us. It's what happens when you're the youngest sibling." Osian shrugged.

"Olivia doesn't throw tantrums."

"Olivia could rule the world riding a unicorn with a tiara on her head." Osian picked up his stack of notebooks and carried them over to the bookshelf. "And she doesn't have a complex like Rolly does."

The detectives arrived an hour later. They were both grumbling about traffic and the weather. The skies had opened up yet again; not a surprise given they lived in London.

They'd brought one of their technicians to check out the laptop. She quickly bagged it up, insisting on taking it to her forensics lab. Osian surprisingly didn't protest when she disappeared out the door with his precious computer.

"Hope you cleared your web browser history," Dannel teased.

"Nothing on the internet is ever completely deleted." Detective Inspector Khan shook his head at them. "How long have you been getting these messages?"

Leaving Osian to answer questions about the messages, Dannel went over to make another pot of tea. He needed to do something with his hands to keep from fidgeting.

The detectives jotted down all the information Osian gave them. Dannel didn't really have anything to add to the conversation. He tried to avoid the intense gazes of both Powell and Khan.

He waited patiently for them to talk about releasing Joel Brown. It was the point of their visit. The emails from the stalker had been a distraction at best.

Every time Dannel thought the detectives would run out of questions, they thought up one more. He didn't think they'd ever get around to telling them about Joel.

Just when they seemed about to get around to it, someone knocked on their door. He glanced over at Osian. The banging became more insistent in the time it took him to answer.

"Chris?" Dannel blinked in surprise at him. He had his hand lifted in preparation to continue banging. "What are you doing here?"

Chris pushed by Dannel into the flat. He came up short when he noticed the detectives. "Ah. Good. This makes things easier."

"What are you talking about?" Dannel closed the door quietly behind him. He skirted around Chris and returned to stand beside Osian. "Make what easier?"

"I know who the killer is."

"I know who the killer is," Chris blurted out. He hesitated for a moment. "Or, it might be more accurate to say I've got an idea that might narrow down your pool of suspects."

In the stunned silence following Chris's dramatic announcement, Osian wondered if he was about to confess to being the killer. It seemed unlikely. The past few weeks, though, had taught him life tended to be stranger than fiction.

"Why don't we all sit down?" Detective Inspector Khan gestured toward the kitchen table. "Or perhaps you'd prefer to come down to the station with us?"

Chris moved over to the table. He nodded his head toward Osian. "He deserves answers."

With a sinking feeling in the pit of his stomach,

Osian sat down beside Dannel, who immediately reached out to take his hand. Chris was the last one to sit down. He reached into his pocket, pulled out his wallet, and opened it to show a photo.

Osian's breath caught in his throat, staring down at the image of a woman who looked startlingly familiar. "Who?"

"Josie Lloyd." Chris pocketed his wallet. "She and her sister were caught up in the same accident as Helena Brown. They were trapped in their car. Georgina went in the first ambulance and survived her injuries. My Josie didn't make it. Died on the way to the hospital."

"You never told me." Osian had never met Chris's girlfriend.

Detective Inspector Powell leaned forward with her elbows on the table. "This gives you motive."

"There's more." Chris rubbed his hands together before finally crossing his arms. "I never imagined they'd actually go this far."

"Who is they?" Detective Inspector Khan prompted when Chris fell silent. "I am considering taking this down to the station to get this conversation on record."

Osian stretched his leg out to nudge Chris with his foot under the table. He knew if the detectives took him to the station, they might never hear the full story. "Well?"

"It started as a support group for those who lost family in the accident. Some of the survivors joined in as well." Chris leaned back into the chair. "We had good intentions. Grieving with a group of people who understand your loss helps more than you can imagine. And then Georgina and Joel became close."

"Close?"

"They seemed to become stuck in the anger stage of grieving. I think they fed off each other's rage." Chris rubbed his forehead. He seemed conflicted by having to share such personal information. "After a few months, our group splintered off into Georgina and Joel against everyone else. I initially joined them because I wanted to support Josie's sister."

"But?" Osian had an idea he knew where this was going.

"As they became more erratic, I tried to talk them around." Chris shook his head. "I should've contacted the police, I suppose. All I had were suspicions. Not even enough to start an investigation."

"Were they behind all those stalker messages?" Dannel asked in a lull in the conversation.

"Stalker messages?" Chris queried.

"Emails. They've been coming into our podcast

inbox. We were going to mention them." Osian stretched the truth slightly. "They vary from odd to vaguely threatened to disturbing. I've kept all of them."

"Our forensics team is continuing to trace the messages." Detective Inspector Khan tried to focus the conversation back on Chris's story. "Tell us why you became suspicious."

"Joel and Georgina both spoke quite fervently about their belief that the paramedics caused the deaths of their loved ones." Chris held his hand up to stop Osian from speaking. "I know it wasn't your fault, mate. I've never believed you did anything but your absolute best. Those two wanted someone to blame. They were never going to be happy without a target for their rage."

"Gemma and Ossie being the perfect targets." Dannel's fingers tightened around Osian's. "Was it simply a coincidence they got her first? Did they mean to kill both of them? Anyone in our circle knows he's part of the first responder cosplay group. We have an Instagram account. We don't make a secret of it."

"I don't know." Chris shrugged. "Georgina was at the Olympia. I saw her. I imagine Joel was around, but I never spotted him. I didn't want to believe either of them were involved in Gemma's murder, but I don't believe in coincidences with everything else that's happened. They've both been stalking Osian. I've followed them a number of times."

"The theatre." Osian remembered finding his sudden appearance strange. "One of them poisoned us."

"Georgina—I think." Chris shifted in the chair uncomfortably. "I adored Josie. I tried to watch out for her sister. I failed miserably. I was following them that night. They disappeared into the theatre, and I suspected they might do something stupid."

"That's why you stood up Abra." Osian hoped his friend would feel better about the situation if Chris proved to be truly innocent. "Did they send the Nandos?"

"I can't say for certain." Chris glanced over at the two detectives. "I imagine you'll be able to narrow your search."

"I'm going to insist you come with us to formalise your statement." Detective Inspector Khan got to his feet. He focused on Osian and Dannel briefly. "Please stay in your flat. Don't take any more unnecessary risks. If he's right, they've no interest in stopping until they've gotten a hold of you."

With those words of warning, the detectives escorted Chris from their flat. Osian locked the door, then rested his forehead against the wood. Dannel joined him, wrapping his arms around Osian from behind.

"This is *not* your fault." Dannel brushed a kiss against the back of Osian's neck. "Don't let this ruin all the progress you've made. You did everything possible to save lives that day."

"I know." He twisted around in Dannel's arms. "Have I mentioned I love you?"

"We're not going outside." Dannel eyed him suspiciously. "Are we?"

Osian grinned at him. "Don't you want to see how Ian is doing?"

"I want to keep anyone else from getting hurt. I don't think our presence at the hospital will do anything to help Ian." Dannel led him away from the front door. "Why don't we record the podcast? It'll keep us both out of trouble."

"Spoilsport."

Grabbing a bag of crisps from the cupboard, Osian snagged two bottles of ale as well. They got comfortable in the living room to finalise the script for their podcast. He was glad he didn't only keep notes on his laptop, since the detectives had it.

"Do you think Chris was involved in Gemma's death?" Dannel twirled a pen in his fingers anxiously.

"He could be throwing Georgina and Joel under the bus to save himself."

Osian leaned against the sofa cushion and tilted his head to stare up at the ceiling. "I want to believe he told the complete truth. How did we not know about his girlfriend?"

"Maybe her parents didn't approve of him? He's always been a private person. Not everyone wants to scream from the rooftops about the love of their life." Dannel dragged the weighted blanket off the arm of the couch to wrap around himself. "Think Abra will forgive him? Given he stood her up to save us?"

"Maybe?" Osian fished his phone out of his pocket when it beeped. He quickly read through the text. "Ian's alert and awake. He's not amused by the hospital aesthetics, apparently, but pleased to have saved our lives. He's open to a monetary reward."

"And dramatic as ever." Dannel bent forward to read the message for himself. "Maybe we should take his favourite croissants to him once he's released?"

"He'll be thrilled while also complaining we're trying to fatten him up." Osian replied to the message, then tossed his phone onto the coffee table. "Wonder if they'll tell us what exactly made him sick?"

"Doubtful. They wouldn't give us details on the poison in our drinks." Dannel reclined back against the sofa. "What if I quit fighting fires full-time? I get requests to create pieces for cosplay all the time. I could open commissions for it and volunteer at the station. Check gear. Run training for new firefighters. I don't want to throw in the towel completely."

"But it's not fulfilling anymore?"

"Maybe." Dannel tugged the weighted blanket more tightly around his body. "I can't stop thinking about Ian."

"Me too."

"Maybe we should go to the hospital?"

Osian didn't think Dannel honestly wanted to go. He was showing all the usual signs of reaching the end of his social rope. "I think you want musical silence and a dark room."

Dannel shrugged uncomfortably.

"Why don't we wait a few hours and see how you feel? Ian might get out of the hospital sooner, and we'd miss him on our way there." Osian thought the detectives and everyone else might be furious with them for being so cavalier with their safety. "He's not going anywhere."

"He'll be going home."

"I swear you pick the most random times to be pedantic about words." Osian snickered with Dannel, who trailed off with a sigh. He reached out to pat him on the leg. "Why don't I turn on the music and close the curtains? It's bright in here."

Taking Dannel's silence as a yes, Osian hopped off the couch. He went over to close the curtains and frowned, looking through the window across the street. A person in a hoodie disappeared into the bookshop.

Had they seen him? Been watching? Osian yanked the curtains shut; he hated how paranoid this had made him.

Queuing up one of their favourite musical theatre soundtracks, Osian decided to head down to check on Ian's flat. He knew Dannel would appreciate being alone. No matter how close they were, some days, he needed time to himself.

It was likely part of why Dannel had begun to seriously consider changing careers: the constant sound, along with forced social interactions. Anyone who worked as a first responder had to deal with people on practically an hourly basis.

"And what are you doing? Little monster." Osian crouched down to catch Thames when the Yorkie tried to race by him on the stairs. "Did you escape?"

"Hello, ducky. Everything all right?" Adelle waved to him. She had Thames's harness in her hand. "He raced out before I could get a hold of the wee creature."

"Here you go. You two be careful, okay?" Osian didn't want to go into details. He just wanted all of the members of their building community to be cautious. "The police aren't sure what might happen next after what happened with Ian."

It wasn't really a lie. The police might believe the killer or killers intended to go after Osian. But they didn't know for certain if someone else might wind up in the crosshairs again.

I will not feel guilty. I don't deserve what's happening. This is not my fault.

Maybe if I repeat it long enough, I'll finally believe myself.

"Would you mind walking Thames for me?" Adelle brought his attention back to her wiggling dog. "I'm not feeling quite myself today."

"Love to." Osian had always considered it their job to help the older tenants any way they could. "Hand Thames over. I'll wear the little bugger out for you."

30

DANNEL

Midway through the fourth repeat of the playlist, a constant banging from the front door of the building drew Dannel out of his happy bubble. He trudged downstairs, waving off Stanley, who'd poked his head out. A young woman held a struggling Thames in her arms.

"Is he yours? I found him sitting outside the door. He got quite cross when I tried to take him away." She held Thames out toward him. "Does he belong here?"

"He's my neighbour's." Dannel adjusted Thames more comfortably in his arms. "Thank you."

After waiting for her to leave, Dannel took the panting dog down the hall to his home. He knocked and waited patiently for either Adelle or Stanley. The former answered with a confused look on her face.

"Did you join Osian on the walk?" She gently plucked Thames out of his arms. "He's had quite a long one today, given when you left."

"What are you talking about?" Dannel didn't even bother to sound polite. "Didn't you lose him?"

"No, I asked your Osian to walk him. I've been a bit peaky for the last few days. And my Stanley had gone out." Adelle unhooked Thames's leash and set him on the floor. "Did Osian not bring him home?"

"Someone found Thames sitting outside the building."

"Oh." Adelle's hand went up to her mouth. "Oh, dear. I hope he hasn't been hurt."

Or worse.

"Stay inside. Keep your door locked." Dannel raced up the stairs, ignoring Adelle's calling after him. He needed to get to his phone. "Stay calm. Stay calm. Stay calm."

First, Dannel tried reaching Osian. He called and texted, waiting a few minutes for a response. Osian would never ignore him.

Ever.

Stay calm.

No matter how many times Dannel repeated the phase. He could feel his blood pressure shooting through the roof. His fingers fumbled with the touch screen on his phone, trying to find Detective Inspector Khan's number.

Answer, you absolute wanker. Answer.

"DI Khan."

"Osian hasn't come home. He's not answering his phone. Something's wrong." Dannel's words ran into one another. He tried to get as much information across as possible. "You have to find him."

"Dannel. Please. I need you to take a few deep breaths. It seems impossible, but you can do it. Just in and out, count the seconds." Detective Inspector Khan had an incredibly calming voice. "We're on our way to your building. Stay there. When did you see him last?"

"I don't know. I don't know." Dannel was panicking. He knew it wouldn't help at all, so he made himself take a few additional deep breaths. "I lay down to rest. He went downstairs to check Ian's apartment. Our neighbour Adelle asked him to walk their dog. Thames, he's her Yorkie, was sitting outside our front door. Maybe the CCTV footage can tell you when Thames came home."

"We'll be there as soon as we can."

After hanging up, Dannel texted Olivia and Roland. Their siblings would handle the news better than their mums. He messaged Fire Chief Wilson to see if Evie might be able to come help in the search.

No matter what the detectives said, Dannel wouldn't sit around and wait. Osian was in danger. He had every intention of making sure the person he loved most in the world came home to him safe and sound.

By the time the detectives arrived, their flat had begun to fill up. Stanley had come from downstairs. Olivia and Drystan had shown up together with his brother Roland following not long after.

"Chief?" Dannel stared blankly when he opened the door to find a large number of his fellow firefighters crammed into the hallway. "Shouldn't you be at the station?"

"We've got our calls covered for the next few hours. Where are we searching?" He disregarded Dannel's bewildered muttering. "You're our family, son. We're here to help; just point us in a direction."

Stepping aside to let them into the flat, Dannel acknowledged the detective who came in behind them. He had several constables behind him. He didn't know how to handle so many people squashed into his place, all focusing their attention on him.

"DI Powell is downstairs with your uncle. They're going over the CCTV footage to see when Osian left and when the dog showed up without him." Detective Inspector Khan came over to stand next to

Dannel. "Once we know the time he left and the direction, we can use other cameras to hopefully locate him."

Abra came rushing through the still open door before Dannel could respond to the detective. She peered around at the gathered crowd before rushing over. "It's not just Oz. Chris isn't answering my texts or calls."

"He did stand you up."

Abra rolled her eyes and waved her phone in his face. "We talked last night. He explained everything. I called him after you mentioned Osian going missing and haven't heard anything."

Dannel's gaze went from Abra to the detective. He hoped their instincts about Chris weren't about to be proven wrong. "Maybe he's ghosting you again?"

"Thought about that. So I called his office and spoke with his boss. He didn't want to answer, but I explained the situation with Osian. His boss called and texted him—Chris didn't respond." Abra grabbed Dannel's hand. "He's not going to ghost his job and risk getting fired."

"What do we do?" Dannel turned toward the detective. He was out of his depth. "Can we search for him?"

"I'd prefer you stay here."

Dannel stared at the man. "They went after Ossie, not me. I can't sit on my arse while he's in danger."

The next thirty minutes went by so quickly yet dragged on painfully at the same time. The detectives managed to track Osian on CCTV cameras. With another word of warning, they headed out, leaving a solitary constable in the hallway.

"I can't *just* stand here." Dannel paced the flat anxiously in what small space was left with the gathered crowd. "I'm going to see my uncle."

"You're not supposed to leave, sir."

Dannel stared at the young constable, raising his eyebrow. "I'll be in the shop downstairs, unless you intend to arrest me."

"Sir."

Ignoring the constable, Dannel jogged down the stairs. He didn't glance behind him to see who had followed. His uncle was scanning through CCTV footage when he stepped into the office at the back of the shop.

"Dan, sweetheart." His auntie came over to wrap him tightly in a hug. "We've called your mum and Osian's mum. They're waiting anxiously together. Now, how can we help?"

"Which way did he go?" Dannel gently extracted himself from his auntie. He didn't want physical contact. The world already felt as though it was closing in on him. "Uncle Danny."

"I shouldn't." His uncle hesitated before playing the video of Osian heading down the street with a jaunty Thames trotting at his feet. "He had to be heading toward Phoenix Garden."

"Thank you."

Without another word, Dannel rushed out of the shop. He jogged down the street, not knowing what he expected to find. It just helped to be doing something.

"Will you slow down?"

"No."

"We don't all have long legs," Abra complained.

Adjusting his pace slightly, Dannel waited for Abra, Evie, and Drystan to catch up with him. He wasn't overly surprised to see Osian's brother-in-law had decided to join them. Olivia had stayed behind.

"She's organising search groups with your fire chief." Drystan grinned at him. "You know my Olivia. She'll have Covent Garden completely covered by searchers in under five seconds."

Dannel didn't have it in him to smile. He simply nodded and picked up his pace again, only stopping when they arrived at the main entrance. "We'll split up and scour the garden. Evie, with me?"

His best friend immediately stepped over to him. She reached down to take his hand. "We'll find him."

"No lying." Dannel didn't want to believe the worst but knew the odds might not be in their favour. "How many close calls do we get before someone else winds up like Gemma?"

"Chris has gone missing, as well. Could they be together?" Evie took one side of the walking path, and Dannel took the other. Their eyes scanned the ground for any clues. "They're both capable of defending themselves."

"Chris's presence might be comforting or terrifying. The jury's still out." Dannel wanted to believe their friend had been truthful with them. He wasn't always the best person to sniff out a liar. "Gemma had a black belt. She knew how to defend herself. Knowledge and ability aren't always a guarantee."

"I'm trying to think happy thoughts."

Dannel squeezed between two bushes to check along the edge of the wrought iron fencing. "Think happy thoughts quietly, then. If I don't get my hopes up, it might not hurt so much when everything comes crashing down."

"Dan."

He waved off Evie's concern and crouched down to peer through two of the iron rods. "What's that?"

Evie joined him by the fence. "I don't see anything."

"Over there by the red door." Dannel pointed to the building adjacent to the garden. "Is that a phone? The case looks like Ossie's."

"Shit."

Racing through the garden to the side entrance, they skidded to a stop by the phone. Evie stopped him from picking it up and immediately called one of the detectives. She didn't want them to destroy any potential fingerprint or DNA evidence.

In case they needed it to identify a killer.

It was her unspoken reason. Dannel tried very hard not to follow her train of thought to the logical conclusion. They waited impatiently for the police to arrive.

"There's another one." Dannel pointed to a glinting screen a few feet away. "Wonder if it's Chris's phone."

"Easy way to tell." Abra and Drystan had caught up to them. She pulled her own mobile out and dialled Chris's number. They waited with bated breath and collectively groaned when a familiar *Star Wars* tune rang out. "Oh, god. Someone kidnapped both of them."

"Or Chris tossed his to keep the GPS from being

tracked." Drystan said what Dannel had been thinking. Abra punched him on the arm. "You can't assume innocence based on an abandoned phone."

Dannel sat on the ground with his back to the wall. He couldn't stop staring at Osian's phone. "Ossie's too careful to drop his mobile. And he'd *never* leave Thames to walk home on his own."

The police arrived, disrupting the conversation. Detective Inspector Khan frowned disapprovingly at Dannel, who ignored him. He pulled a glove onto his hand and then picked up Osian's phone.

"Do you know the passcode?" he asked after trying to turn it on. "Let's make sure this is the right phone."

"It's my birthday." Dannel gave it to the man. "I'll make him change it."

"I'm hurt you don't trust us to not take advantage." Abra tried to lighten the mood. Her smile evaporated when the passcode worked. "Damn. I'd hoped it wasn't his phone."

Waking up with a splitting headache wasn't an entirely new experience for Osian. He'd worked long hours as a paramedic after all. That his wrists had been secured together with a plastic cable tie was a first.

"What the sodding hell is going on?" He groaned.

"Keep your voice down."

"I was." Osian tried to sit up and assess the situation. He'd been lying on his side on a hard concrete floor. "Chris? That you?"

Rolling over, Osian carefully eased himself up into a seated position. He leaned back against a wall to keep from tipping over again. His head was pounding, and waves of dizziness kept threatening to cause him to fall over.

"Over here."

"Helpful." Osian squinted in the badly lit room—even the minimal light seemed too bright for him—eventually spotting his friend secured to a radiator. "How stereotypical of them."

"Now do you believe me?"

"Is this really the time for an 'I told you so,' Chris? Wanker." Osian tried to carefully assess his body for any injuries. He breathed through a bout of nausea. "Are you hurt? How did we get here?"

"You sent me a message to meet you at the park. When I arrived, you were on the ground. The little dog you were walking took off. Joel and Georgina were there. I tried to talk them down, but I didn't want to risk you getting struck again." Chris kept his voice low and kept shooting glances toward the door at the far end of the room. "I figured we had a better chance of survival together."

"I didn't send you a message." Osian repeated his question since Chris hadn't answered. "Are you hurt?"

"I'm fine. More concerned about you."

"I definitely have a concussion." Osian had treated enough of them to be well-versed on the symptoms. "Why haven't they simply killed us?"

"Careful what you wish for," he muttered. "Can you get your hands free?"

Osian stared down at the plastic tie securing his wrists together. "No?"

"Listen. Here's what I need you to do." Chris tried yanking at the handcuffs securing him to the radiator. "Twist your wrists so they're pressed together. Grab the free end of the tie with your teeth and tighten it as far as you can."

"Tighten it?"

"Trust me, please?" Chris whispered urgently. "We don't have much time."

"All right, all right."

They kept a close eye on the door while Osian tried to shift his wrists around. He managed to get a hold of the edge of the tie with his teeth and yank on it. They held their breaths when they heard raised voices.

"Shit. What next?"

"Raise your hands over your head, widen your elbows out as far as you can get them, and bring your arms down with all the force you can muster. You want your wrists to put a strain against the plastic, so pull your arms out." Chris shifted again, pulling himself up slightly. "It might hurt."

Bugger.

I have to do this.

I can do this.

Bugger.

"Go on," Chris encouraged.

"Right." Osian used all the force he could muster to thrust his arms down. "Holy mother of spies. It worked."

"Holy mother of spies?"

"I'm dizzy. Leave me alone." Osian stared down at the broken plastic. "But seriously, were you some kind of secret agent in a second life and didn't bother to tell me? Should I be cosplaying as you instead of Nathan Drake?"

"Breathe through the adrenaline." Chris ignored his whispered rambling, which was probably a good idea. "How are your wrists doing?"

It did hurt. Not as bad as his head whenever he moved even an inch. He flexed his fingers and rolled his wrists, trying to regain feeling and ease the sting from snapping the plastic tie.

"Oz? Your wrists?" Chris prompted when he fell silent. "Can you come over here?"

"They're doing better than my head." Osian tried to get to his feet, but his legs buckled. His vision swam. "Bugger. Definitely concussed."

Staying on his knees, Osian shuffled slowly across the room. He fought off another bout of nausea. Moving was not helping.

"Osian?"

"Shh." Osian sat on his heels and covered his ears. He knew Chris had kept his voice low, but it felt as though he were shouting. "Unless you want whatever's in my stomach all over you. How long have we been captive?"

"We need to get you to the hospital." Chris lowered his voice even further.

"Well, sure, let's just walk out of here. Oh, wait. You're handcuffed to a sodding radiator. There are two murderous wankers on the other side of the door. And I can't even get to my feet without the room spinning," Osian snarked. He reached to carefully feel around his head, checking for the sore spot and for any blood. "Don't you have any handy tricks for getting yourself free?"

"You don't happen to have a hairpin? Or a paperclip?"

"Oh, sure." Osian rolled his eyes, then regretted it immediately. "I always carry around paperclips."

"Why don't you see if you can find a bit of wire or a piece of metal—something the size of a paperclip?" Chris kept watching him with concern obvious in his eyes. "Your pupils are dilated."

"Differently sized? Or equally dilated?"

"Equally."

"Let me know if they change." Osian knew his pupils being dilated wasn't necessarily directly related to his head injury. They needed to keep an eye on it. *Pun intended.* "I definitely need to get to the hospital."

Glancing around the room, Osian spotted a pile of rubbish. He made his way over to it. *Who just throws their bags of trash into their basement? The same wankers who take people hostage.*

"Careful."

And by careful, Osian knew Chris meant quiet. Their captors were still arguing upstairs. He kept an ear out just in case the raised voices stopped.

Or came closer.

Digging through the trash was almost too much for his already wobbly tummy. Osian foraged in the rubbish and came out with a pen, two bent paperclips, and a strip of metal about the length of his finger. He hoped Chris could play MacGyver and rescue himself.

Osian shuffled his way over to him and offered up his bounty on the palm of his hand. "Okay, Houdini."

"He died trying to escape."

"Hope we have better luck than he did." Osian wanted to lie down and close his eyes. He knew staying awake was critically important. "What now?"

Chris took the thin strip of metal and folded it in half. He slipped it into one of the cuffs, along the rim, pushing it forward with the restraint, which clicked. "There. First one down. Let me get the second off me."

"What the—" Osian stared at him in disbelief. "You're teaching me how to do that when we get out of here. Wicked party trick. You're two for two. This is the worst escape room in history."

"They're going to stop arguing eventually." Chris had gotten to his feet. He pocketed the cuffs and walked slowly around the room. "Can you swing a weapon?"

"What about my inability to stand makes you think I'm capable of defending myself?"

"We're not dying in a dank basement. So you might have to." Chris dug around in the trash, coming out with the remnants of a broken mop. He found a second one in the corner. "I have an idea."

"This is usually the point in crime shows where everything goes horribly wrong." Osian tried to stand again. He managed with less of a wobble. "What's the plan?"

"We're going to bank on them being inexperienced." Chris looped an arm around Osian and helped him over to the door. "Crouch by here. We're going to play on the element of surprise. If you can trip up the second person to enter, I'm confident I can disarm the first. We want extra time to avoid dealing with them simultaneously."

"Glad someone's confident."

Movies and television made suspense-filled moments intense, with sweeping musical scores and dramatic cinematography. Osian thought they definitely needed drums and a full orchestra. He also wanted to be played by someone in better shape who knew some form of self-defence.

They'd also failed to prepare him for how boring waiting for the baddies could be. Osian was struggling to keep his eyes open. He kept himself awake by singing his favourite *Hamilton* song under his breath.

"They've stopped arguing," Chris whispered. He'd taken a spot on the other side of the door. "Stay awake, Oz."

"Doing my best."

Voices drew closer. Osian didn't recognise either the man or the woman. He'd only heard Joel Brown once before and couldn't recall having heard Georgina; he had no memory of being attacked by them at the park.

The door creaked open. If they'd been in a horror film, Osian thought this would've been the moment when the monster revealed themselves for the first time. He stayed hidden in the darkness and watched Georgina move down the stairs.

When Joel followed a second later, Osian managed to hold out the broken broom in time to trip him up. The man catapulted off the steps. He went headfirst, tumbling straight into the back of Georgina, sending them both crashing to the floor on top of each other. A comedic end to what had been a terrifying wait.

Osian wanted to laugh at the absurdity of the moment. "Think they're more Mr Bean than serial killers."

"We're not free yet," Chris cautioned. He held his cuffs loosely in one hand and went for Joel. "Keep an eye on her."

Showing an impressive amount of skill and familiarity with restraint, Chris had Joel on his stomach with his wrists cuffed behind his back within a second. Osian got unsteadily to his feet and leaned against the wall. Georgina had managed to roll away from her partner in crime and surged up as well.

"You bastard." She lunged toward him.

Osian squinted at her. Her shouting was only serving to make his headache worse. "Chris."

"I've got her." He left Joel on the ground and intercepted Georgina before she reached Osian. "What were you thinking? Josie would never have wanted you to do this."

"Me?" Georgina swung at Chris, who easily deflected her punch. "I told him we should've brought the gun down with us. He wanted to gloat."

"Villains." Osian shook his head. He smiled when Chris glared at him. "What? Every bad guy in every movie has to gloat."

Chris ignored him and focused on Georgina. "What was the grand plan? Kill both of us? What on earth possessed you?"

"They *murdered* my sister. Even if you didn't love her enough to make them pay, I did. Joel did. His poor wife. What about her?" Georgina continued to struggle in his grasp. "I thought you understood."

"My Josie died in a tragic accident. Nothing Osian or any of the paramedics did or didn't do could've changed anything. The accident caused her death. Not them. You don't get to turn her passing into some bizarre crusade." Chris grabbed her arms more tightly, holding her away from him when she tried for a kick. "Oz? Can you hear me?"

"Yeah?" Osian forced his eyes open. He was really starting to struggle to stay conscious. "Chris? I think I need to sit down. My head's hurting worse."

And this would be the stage when I rushed a patient to the hospital.

Staying upright seemed an almost impossible task. Osian tried to lock his knees. He didn't want to pass out on Chris, leaving him alone with Georgina and Joel.

"Oz? One of us needs to head upstairs to try to call the police. They have to be searching for us by now. These two aren't clever enough to have covered their tracks completely." Chris came closer, holding Georgina away from Osian, since she continued to struggle. "Hey. Osian. Focus on my voice."

"I'm not going toward the light." Osian sat down heavily when the room began spinning more than it had earlier. "Not good. Very much, not good."

"Osian." Chris snapped his fingers repeatedly. "*Oz.*"

Osian tried hard to keep his eyes open. He tilted his head to the side when the nausea become too much for him. "Chris. Where's the ambulance?"

"Just hang on, yeah? You're going to be fine. We need to call the police to let them know where we are."

The last hour had gone by in a haze. Dannel had developed tunnel vision, focusing entirely on the detectives who were waiting for the department's CCTV operators to locate where Osian and Chris had been taken. He'd refused to be taken home; not without answers.

Not without Osian.

From one second to the next, the detectives' energy changed rapidly. Detective Inspector Khan had taken a call. He'd spoken urgently into his phone while several other officers hovered around him.

"I'm going with you." Dannel forced himself to hold eye contact with the detective. "You've found him."

"We might—"

"You've found him." Dannel cut off the detective before he could put him off. "I heard you. You're all preparing to rush out. You wouldn't do that unless there was concrete information."

He considered Dannel briefly before eventually nodding. "Fine. Come on, then. You're in the car with me."

They drove through familiar streets and finally stopped at the end of a street across from a row of houses. Dannel thought they appeared so ordinary. Detective Inspector Khan warned him to stay in the vehicle.

Despite nodding his agreement, Dannel climbed out of the back of the unmarked car the moment the police had breached the front door. He waited impatiently, trying to peer inside the house. What was taking so long?

He knew from being called out to fires involving police arrests that they were noisy. Always. He worried what the absolute silence coming from inside the house meant.

A crackle on the radio in the vehicle drew his attention. The detectives were calling for an ambulance. Paramedics. *Who's hurt?* Dannel was suddenly imagining the worst.

He started across the street and stared down the

constable who tried to stop him. "I won't go inside until the house is clear."

He might.

The constable didn't have to know.

Agonising seconds later, Detective Inspector Powell led out Joel Brown. His hands were cuffed behind his back. She left him in the hands of several constables and returned inside.

Georgina Lloyd came out next. She struggled against the officer. They dragged her down the pavement, cursing the entire way.

With both of the suspects secured safely, Dannel rushed up the stairs into the house. He rushed through room after room before following Detective Inspector Khan's voice to a narrow set of stairs. The man shook his head disapprovingly when Dannel joined them in the basement.

Dannel didn't hear a word the detective said, his entire being focused on the limp body stretched out prone on the floor. "*Ossie.*"

Chris caught him by the arms when his knees threatened to go out from under him. "He's alive. Just suffering from a concussion."

"Just suffering from a concussion?" Dannel knew how dangerous head trauma could be. "Where's the sodding ambulance?"

"Ortea. Haven't heard your lovely dulcet tones in a while. Why don't you back up and allow us to check on our patient?" Freya Davies eased him out of the way with her bag. "Make room, lads. We're bringing in a spine board to allow us to get him up the steps and onto a stretcher."

Some of the fear in his heart eased at the confidence from Freya. She was one of Osian's good friends and Abra's ex-girlfriend. They'd remained close and ran the LGBTQIA+ first responders coalition together.

"Dan. Breathe. He's going to be fine." Freya spoke over her shoulder. She coordinated the efforts of the four other paramedics in the room. "We'll take excellent care of our boy."

His hands trembled too much for him to offer any assistance in carrying the stretcher. He simply watched. Chris stepped up beside him; he was holding a broken broomstick in his hand.

"Are you hurt?" Dannel gave him a once-over.

"I'm fine."

"He'll be coming along with us for a thorough check over or Abs will never forgive me." Freya stared pointedly at Chris until he followed after her. "We'll meet you at the hospital, Dan. I'll take good care of them both."

Within minutes, the paramedics had disappeared

with their two patients. Dannel stared around the room in shock. He crouched down to pick up a broken cable tie from the floor. Had Chris or Osian been kept captive with it?

"Mr Ortea?"

Dannel knew the detective had spoken. He couldn't process the words. His fingers closed around the plastic strips. "Sorry. What?"

"Mr... Dannel." Detective Inspector Khan came over to him. He gently removed the cable ties from his hand, placing them into an evidence bag. "Let's get you to the hospital. The scene can't be processed with you here."

Despite nodding his agreement, Dannel didn't know if his feet were capable of moving. He reminded himself Osian was alive. Maybe not conscious, but he'd definitely been breathing when they carried him up the stairs.

"Come on, son."

Dannel glanced up in confusion at the familiar voice. "Chief?"

"Davies thought you might want a friendly face to get you to the hospital. Your brother's waiting." He walked over and wrapped an arm around Dannel's shoulder. "Let's get out of the detective's hair."

The hand on his shoulder guided him up the

stairs, through the house, and into the chaos of outside. Officers had cordoned off the street. He wasn't overly surprised to see a crowd of onlookers.

"Rolly." Dannel spotted his brother waiting for them. "Rolly."

"Easy, big brother." Roland came over to give him a hug. "Inside voice. Let's not give the crowd a show."

Dannel didn't get a chance to respond. His brother shoved him into the back seat. "Did you call Mum? What about Ossie's family?"

"Texted Liv the second I arrived. They're all gathering at the hospital. Prepare yourself for hugs. You're going to be smothered." Roland reached back to pat him on the leg. "Breathe."

"Will you wankers stop telling me that? I haven't suddenly forgotten to inhale and exhale." Dannel yanked the seat belt across his body, shoving the clip in to secure it. "I'm not magically calming down because you remind me to breathe."

"Inside voice."

"Use your own damn inside voice." Dannel flicked his finger against his leg repeatedly. He was teetering on the edge of a meltdown and desperately trying not to do so. Being agitated in a hospital wouldn't help anyone. "Just leave me alone for a bit, all right?"

Instead of responding, Roland pulled his phone

out. He connected the Bluetooth, and seconds later one of the tracks from *In The Heights* began to play, a cast album both Dannel and his brother had enjoyed greatly.

They'd connected with the idea of being the children of immigrants even if they weren't living in New York City. London was big and metropolitan. It hadn't been that much of a stretch to them when the play had come out.

"We're here."

Dannel had lost himself in the music. One full playthrough of the album usually helped him bleed off the energy; he barely had time for a couple songs before they arrived at the hospital. Neither his brother nor Chief Wilson commented or complained about him singing at the top of his lungs. "I don't know if I can go inside."

"Of course you can." Roland slid out of the front seat and came around to open the passenger door. "I'll help."

Staring at his brother's hand, Dannel waved him off and climbed out of the back seat. He stood up to his full height and inhaled a ragged, painful breath. The hospital loomed in front of them, more terrifying than it had been the last time he'd been here with Ian.

Between his brother and Chief Wilson, Dannel

made it through the hospital to the small waiting room where their family and friends had gathered. They'd been in A & E more in the past month than in the last few years. Dannel hoped the arrest of Joel and Georgina would bring an end to the trend.

"Where is he?" Dannel ignored the questions thrown at him by everyone.

Olivia caught him by the hand and pointed toward the first room on the right. "The doctors just finished up with tests. They're waiting for him to wake naturally. They believe he's going to be okay. There wasn't any bleeding on the brain. He's going to be okay."

Sidestepping both of their mums, Dannel snuck into the room. He didn't care if they were supposed to wait outside. Osian wasn't going to wake up alone.

Dannel closed the door behind him. He eased around the curtain to find Osian hooked up to wires and covered with a blanket. "Ossie."

Quietly shifting one of the chairs in the room next to the bed, Dannel sat down and picked up one of the limp hands. He hated seeing Osian so still. *Why did you go out with Thames on your own? Bloody hell, Ossie.*

"I can hear you complaining about me." Osian opened his eyes enough to squint at Dannel. "Too bright."

"Hang on." Dannel went over to pull the curtains shut, blocking out the rare bit of London sun. "Better?"

"Loads." Osian opened his eyes completely. He gave a tired grin. "Hello, love."

"Ossie." Dannel dropped into the chair with an exhausted grunt. "'Hello, love?' Are you honestly starting with that?"

"Is there a better way to start than with telling you how much I love you?" Osian reached his arm out toward Dannel, gripping his hand tightly. "Particularly when I thought I'd never get to say those words again?"

Dannel rested his forehead against their joined hands. He wanted to crawl into bed with Osian and nap for days, though the doctors probably wouldn't approve. "Next time you run off on an adventure... take me with you."

By the start of April, Osian had completely recovered from his concussion. He'd only stayed in the hospital for one day. They'd released him when all the brain scans came back clear —a great relief to everyone involved.

The police had been busy completing their investigation. They'd had a lot of questions for both Chris and Osian. He'd almost lost his temper being asked the same things in twenty different ways.

After a week or so of being home, Osian had set up their recording equipment. He wanted to get back into the flow of podcasting. They might lose some of their audience if they maintained radio silence for too long.

Instead of covering recent murders in and around London, they went into as much detail as possible about their own recent experiences. Detective Inspector Khan had even volunteered to answer questions on air. It had been their most listened-to episode.

"I'm Danny. He's Osian. This has been another episode of our London Crime Podcast. Be sure to say tuned next week when we interview an expert in personal security for tips and tricks to keep yourself safe." Dannel closed out the hour of talk. He grabbed the bottle next to his notebook for a drink while Osian focused his attention on wrapping up the recording correctly. "Much better than D and Oz."

"Not as hip." Osian grinned at him. "Still can't believe the spymaster agreed to be interviewed."

"Are you ever going to stop calling Chris spymaster?"

Since essentially helping him rescue himself, Chris had become a much closer friend. Abra definitely approved. She'd been overly concerned about his health, much to their amusement.

"You didn't see him slip out of those cuffs. I'm telling you, he's some undercover agent." Osian made sure to save a backup of their recording. He preferred to keep two copies when he worked on editing to avoid a catastrophe. "Our own Jason Bourne. Or Sam Fisher."

"Chris wasn't a government experiment. You're not

allowed to play *Splinter Cell* anymore." Dannel shook his head and laughed. "How's the head?"

He counted to ten silently to keep from getting annoyed. Dannel had asked him the same question at least five times each day since he came from the hospital. "I'm fine. Not even the hint of a headache."

On the one hand, Osian understood the concern. Dannel struggled reading his expression and body language. His only way to make sure Osian was actually okay would be to ask questions.

So, Osian understood. And he did his best to never show frustration. Dannel didn't need to feel bad for being a loving boyfriend.

"Are you ready for court next week?"

Osian heard the hesitance in Dannel's voice. "As ready as I can be. I suppose Georgina and Joel have more reason to be anxious. I'm a victim and a witness. It's their lives at stake."

"Myron wants to go."

Osian tried not to react. He'd been staying out of it while Myron continued to attempt to rebuild his relationship with his son. "And?"

Dannel lifted his shoulders slowly. "I don't know. He's trying."

"We can't stop him from attending court."

"He asked."

Osian appreciated the man being respectful enough not to add unnecessary stress to their lives. "It's up to you, love. I'm not bothered one way or the other."

"I'll think on it."

They'd been kept somewhat informed of the police investigation. Detective Inspector Khan had checked in on them several times since Osian's release from the hospital. He'd come over to share a takeaway with them along with joining them on the podcast.

He was a friend. A stingy one, since he refused to give them all the details of the case. He had told them the villainous duo had been officially charged with Gemma's murder.

Their laptop had been returned the day Osian came home from the hospital. The detectives had retrieved two computers from Joel's place. It had been Georgina's account sending the messages, however.

Osian thought both of them had likely taken turns writing the emails. He didn't care, aside from being thrilled they'd stopped. "Archie's finally responded to our panicked texting."

"Finally?" Dannel paused in the middle of filling the kettle for tea. "Is he okay?"

"Perfectly fine. Confused as to why he had a million text and voice messages." Osian joined him in the kitchen. He leaned against the fridge. "Abs thinks we should throw a welcome home party for him. Maybe also use it as a celebration of life for Gemma."

"Here?" Dannel queried hopefully.

"We'll stick with the first responder cosplay group then. Maybe Chris to keep Abs happy. Plus, we can take the mickey over their adorable romance." Osian had anticipated Dannel wanting to stay close to home. He'd already begun to make plans with Abra and Evie. "Love?"

"Don't."

One of the more tangible impacts of their encounter with two killers had been Dannel's increased desire to isolate. He hadn't even gone to the station once since Osian had come home from the hospital. They'd become hermits.

Chief Wilson had come by to see them. Dannel had talked with the man for a while. He'd essentially transitioned from full-time to a volunteer position, helping around the station instead of going out on calls.

They hoped it would greatly reduce Dannel's stress.

Dannel grabbed the edge of the counter, leaning forward with his head down. "When we go outside, all

I can picture is someone grabbing you and me finding you dead on the ground."

"Anxiety can be a right wanker."

"It's not like when we went out on our shifts and I knew you or I might face difficult and dangerous moments. But it came with the territory of being a first responder." Dannel didn't move when Osian stepped up behind him. "I can't quit thinking about you passed out on the basement floor."

"It's okay, love." Osian wrapped his arms around Dannel and rested his head against his back. "We're going to get through this together."

He had no doubts they would. They'd comfort each other through the continued nightmares. He fully believed they'd heal from the trauma of his kidnapping and their multiple near-death experiences.

"And Ian."

"What?" Osian stepped away when Dannel moved out of his arms to grab the kettle. "What about Ian?"

"Let's invite him to the party," Dannel clarified. "He loves theatre, and our dinners always devolve into musical sing-alongs."

There had been three major changes in their lives after his kidnapping. Dannel had hermitted, Osian had become even more obsessed with true crime, and they'd taken even better care of their neighbours. They checked on Ian daily even though he'd made a full recovery.

"When's Archie coming home?" Dannel swirled the water around in the teapot. "Grab the biscuits?"

"He's already home, actually. Wondered if we wanted to see him before the madness of a party." Osian picked through the packets to find the half-eaten bag of Custard Creams. "He apparently met a guy while on his hike through wherever he was. Another adventurer. They came back to London together. His mum *doesn't* approve."

"Why?" Dannel peeked over his shoulder to look at his phone screen. "Tell Archie to come over. He can bring a pizza."

"We're having tea." Osian spoke around the two biscuits he'd shoved into his mouth. He coughed crumbs when Dannel poked him in the side. "What?"

"Aren't paramedics consumed with cleanliness?" He dropped a cube of sugar into one of the mugs of tea and slid it toward Osian. "Text Archie. See if he wants to come over this evening. We can throw him a party on the weekend."

"You just want all the gossip about his new boyfriend."

"Don't you?"

"True." Osian sent a quick text, then caught Dannel by his shirt to drag him over for a kiss. "I love you."

Dannel carefully set his tea on the counter to avoid scalding either of them. "I love you too. I'm not letting you have my biscuit."

"Selfish prat." Osian dragged his fingers across Dannel's jaw. "Still love you."

***

Craving more mysteries? I have a few for you to be checking out. **Meet Motts and the quirky cast of characters in her world.** *Poisoned Primrose* **is a quintessential cosy British mystery and an all-round fun story to throw yourself into.**

You won't want to miss out on reading my *Grasmere Cottage Mystery* **trilogy. With love, wit, and a murder to solve, life for Valor and Bishan is about to get bloomin' complicated in this sweet gay romance.**

ACKNOWLEDGMENTS

A massive thank you to my brilliant betas who take my first draft and help me turn it into something legible. To Becky and Olivia, who always have faith in me. To all the fantastic people at Hot Tree. And also to my beloved hubby, who keeps me from losing my mind while I'm stressing over word counts.

And, lastly, thank you, readers, for following me on my writing journey. I hope you enjoyed Cosplay Killer. I indulged my nerdy heart in so many ways writing this and had such fun doing it.

ABOUT THE AUTHOR

Dahlia Donovan wrote her first romance series after a crazy dream about shifters and damsels in distress. She prefers irreverent humour and unconventional characters. An autistic and occasional hermit, her life wouldn't be complete without her husband and her massive collection of books and video games.

Join Dahlia's newsletter:
http://eepurl.com/QonoX

Dahlia would love to hear from you directly, too. Please feel free to email her at dahlia@dahliadonovan.com or check out her website dahliadonovan.com for updates.

 facebook.com/dahliadonovan

twitter.com/DahliaDonovan

instagram.com/dahliadonovanauthor

pinterest.com/dahliadonovan

bookbub.com/authors/dahlia-donovan

ALSO BY DAHLIA DONOVAN

THE GRASMERE COTTAGE MYSTERY TRILOGY

Dead in the Garden - Dead in the Pond - Dead in the Shop

MOTTS COLD CASE MYSTERY SERIES

Poisoned Primrose

Pierced Peony

LONDON PODCAST MYSTERY SERIES

Cosplay Killer

STAND-ALONE ROMANCES

After the Scrum

At War With A Broken Heart

Forged in Flood

Found You

One Last Heist

Pure Dumb Luck

Here Comes The Son

All Lathered Up

Not Even A Mouse

The Misguided Confession

THE SIN BIN (COMPLETE SERIES)

The Wanderer - The Caretaker - The Royal Marine -

The Botanist - The Unexpected Santa

The Lion Tamer - Haka Ever After

ABOUT THE PUBLISHER

Hot Tree Publishing opened its doors in 2015 with an aspiration to bring quality fiction to the world of readers. With the initial focus on romance and a wide spread of romance subgenres, Hot Tree Publishing has since opened their first imprint, Tangled Tree Publishing, specializing in crime, mystery, suspense, and thriller.

Firmly seated in the industry as a leading editing provider to independent authors and small publishing houses, Hot Tree Publishing is the sister company to Hot Tree Editing, founded in 2012. Having established in-house editing and promotions, plus having a well-respected market presence, Hot Tree Publishing endeavors to be a leader in bringing quality stories to the world of readers.

Interested in discovering more amazing reads brought to you by Hot Tree Publishing? Head over to the website for information:

www.hottreepublishing.com

facebook.com/hottreepublishing

twitter.com/hottreepubs

instagram.com/hottreepubs

MORE FROM HOT TREE PUBLISHING

Want more great romances? Check out Hot Tree Publishing's collection of mixed-genre romantic reads.

Amy McClung

Ann Grech

Avery Sterling

Carolyn LaRoche

Charyse Allan

Dahlia Donovan

Eden French

Eva King

Gen Ryan

Genevive Chamblee

Heidi Renee Mason

Jas T. Ward

Jackson Kane

Katherine McIntyre

Kolleen Fraser

Krissy V

Laura N. Andrews

Lindsay Detwiler

Mary Billiter

Megan Lowe

ML Nystrom

MV Ellis

Natalina Reis

Samatha Harris

Skye McNeil

Theresa Oliver

Virginia Cantrell

CPSIA information can be obtained
at www.ICGtesting.com
Printed in the USA
LVHW090000270121
677549LV00009B/1697